Praise for *Ferenji*

Finely written and astutely observed. – *Dermot Bolger*

An engaging and highly readable collection.
– *Sarah Gilmartin, Irish Times*

Smart, nuanced, provocative, and so well written.
– *Colum McCann*

A sense of futility pervades the collection – a despair that whatever has been achieved has not been enough.
– *Anne Sexton, HOT PRESS*

Powerful and evocative. – *Martin Doyle, IRISH TIMES*

Daring, complex, original. – *Eamonn Wall*

Mulkerns is a writer to reckon with. –
Sue Leonard, BOOKS IRELAND

An international voice that resonates with a deep empathy.
– *Emer Martin*

Beautifully written and topical. – *Nuala O'Connor*

Her stories concern real people working, often idealists, whose principles, beliefs, are challenged ... by the randomness of war's violence. – *MJ Stephens, RAIN TAXI*

Other books

ferenji

stories from the field

HELENA MULKERNS

451
Editions

December 2022
You've heard
them all before
but here they
are again.
Thanks
for being
there to support
the errant
wanderer
and this book
comes with all
my love, dear
friend - Helena
XX

First published in 2016 by Doire Press, Galway
www.DoirePress.com

2nd edition published by 451 Editions, Dublin
www.451Editions.com

ISBN 978-1-9162975-8-6

Cover image: Helena Mulkerns
Printed in Ireland by Sprintprint, Dublin

The author gratefully acknowledges the assistance of The
Arts Council / An Chomhairle Ealaíon in the writing of this
book.

TABLE OF CONTENTS

Ferenji is a word used to describe foreigners, or invaders, across a wide sweep of the globe. It originates from the historical Persian and Arabic term *farangi,* perhaps itself from the French *francs* (dating from the time of the crusades). Contemporary variations of it are found in native tongues from Ethiopia (*ferenghi*) to India (*firangi*) and Thailand (*falang*), and its meaning, depending on context, can run from affectionate to extremely pejorative.

Author's Note

From 1999 to 2008, Helena Mulkerns worked as a public information officer and photographer for United Nations Peacekeeping Operations in Central America, Africa and Asia. *Ferenji* is a fictional work inspired by personal experiences during that period and all its characters and incidents are invented. Any resemblance in the stories to actual people, organisations or events is purely coincidental.

For my mother, Helen

ferenji

A CHILD CALLED PEACE

Selam pulled her light cotton veil up over her head as the midday sun began to burn her scalp. They were nearly home now. She followed her older brother along the dusty road, watching the line of goats that were dancing behind him, single file. She was sure they were missing one.

'Hassan!' she called.

As usual he was paying no attention to her, playing the important role of boss shepherd and singing a song to the sky as he walked. Even though she was the baby of the family, and a girl, Selam took her own role as assistant shepherd very seriously, and when she counted the animals again, she knew she was right.

She stopped and peered across the landscape, the bright light making it hard to distinguish anything moving on the rocky terrain. They would be in deep trouble if she didn't find it.

She smiled when she finally spotted the missing kid goat, black and chocolate brown, his little tail twitching as he pulled at something under a rock, only a short distance away. She looked at the ground that lay between her feet and the kid's shiny hooves. Mama had told her not to play in this place, but he was out there dancing as gaily as the others.

Making clicking sounds with her tongue, she set off to retrieve him.

The view through the windscreen was familiar by now, but the utter starkness of the desert still managed to impress and terrify the Lieutenant all at once, every time she went out on patrol. Ahead, the heat was rippling up the view, twisting the horizon into a row of drunken amoebas. No clouds at all, just a pristine blue sky arching over the endless sand and rock, as cluttered with the detritus of war as the sky was clear. On both sides of her, she could see a random scattering of spent shells, ammo boxes and nose-dived rockets, with the occasional live mortar peeping from the sand.

They didn't usually travel this late, at the hottest time of the day, but they had been delayed on patrol, checking in at the demining operations 80 kilometres into the Danakil. Although the rebels had been relatively quiet in the area over the previous month, mission regulations required all vehicles to travel in convoys. This morning the vehicle following behind the Hibernian Peacekeepers' truck was a field ambulance belonging to the mission's demining unit, manned by two Slovak medics, Miloš and Karel.

As she drove, Dara nodded at the gaudy red metal signs placed at regular intervals along the road, freshly daubed with white paint, depicting a skull and crossbones.

'Is this the landmine project you were working on last week, Tom?' she asked. To her right, Corporal Thomas Dunne, flaunting regulations as per usual, was puffing on a cigarette.

'Yeah. That Minefree Planet bunch paid for the signs, mostly. A few of their experts were in from Nairobi, so Captain Neary sent us along to give a hand. Biggest minefield in the country.'

'It must have been some battle.'

'The remnants of it. Nasty place.'

'Better than just patrolling up and down the sand dunes.'

'With no fuckan air conditioning.'

They laughed. It was the mission's Irish joke. Logistics had sent the contingent into one of the hottest deserts on earth with vehicles shipped from Bosnia.

'Do you know, when they arrived they all had snow chains?'

'And the fan heaters are great!' Dara spluttered. 'So how's the clearance going around here?'

'Yeah. Well, how long is a piece of string? But at least the roads are demined and the signs are up. They're tryin' to sort some community events — landmine awareness stuff. I volunteered...'

'Good for you.'

'Hey — looka that!'

Dara glanced off the road, where a large animal carcass lay decomposing in the sun.

'We coulda had a barbie, mate!' Tom mimicked the laid-back accent of the Aussie deminers, laughing.

'Ha ha,' Dara said, somewhat flummoxed by the Corporal's untiring cheer. Apart from the routine complaints, he never seemed personally affected by the devastation around them. Since this was her first peacekeeping tour, despite her seniority in rank, she often felt like a novice beside

15

him, with his three years in UWIFIL. He'd visit a refugee camp and jovially give out handfuls of sweeties from his pockets or ballpoint pens to the teenagers, apparently unfazed by the appalling squalor and suffering. Dara almost envied his ability to remain so detached. She felt uncomfortable, even overwhelmed, patrolling through ruined villages or holding camps, yet Tom seemed to just treat it all like a good pensionable job, counting the days to his home leave and listening to the Irish radio station broadcast at the Base, one foot at home and one in a war zone. Maybe that was the best way to be.

They continued at a steady pace, the ambulance following behind them, past the ruins of a bombed-out mosque and some abandoned village dwellings. It was almost thirteen hundred hours when they saw the boy, materialising out of the bleached flat light like a little ghost, waving from the distance where the road met the sky.

'What's that?' Tom asked, squinting.

Dara peered, saw a figure jumping up and down, flailing its arms. The ambulance to the rear honked twice and overtook them.

When they caught up, the medics were trying to catch and calm down a little fella no more than twelve years old. He was screaming at them, his huge eyes flashing with fear, as he ran back and forth to the edge of the road. Blood soaked the front of his T-shirt and shorts. He shouted some more, waved his hands out towards the open desert, repeating one word over and over.

Karel tried to catch hold of him, but he pulled away again, screaming the word between huge breaths.

'Shite,' Tom said. 'We should have an interpreter every time we go out, I keep sayin'...'

Eventually the boy broke free, running straight into the minefield. It was agonising to watch.

'Mines — mines!' Karel screamed.

About twenty metres away, the kid stopped and glanced back. Dara watched as he bent down and began to drag something along the ground towards the soldiers. Karel squinted across the sand and then ran to the back of the ambulance, followed by Miloš.

'Another kid...'

Faces encased in Perspex, blue flak aprons heavy across their torsos and legs, they inched out across the sand towards the boy, panning a metal detector over what they could find of his steps.

Standing at the edge of the road, Dara ran her nails back and forth along the seam of her pockets. For a moment she felt utterly helpless. Then her training took over and she ordered Tom to call it in.

He climbed in the truck and reached for the handset.

'Hotel Tango Delta to Papa Kilo Base 3, over...'

'Papa Kilo Base 3 to Hotel Tango Delta, we copy, over...'

'Reporting civilian landmine casualty, 13:00 hours, kilometre 80 Route 1, over…'

In slow, steady steps the medics made their way back to the vehicles. Tom opened the back of the ambulance. Dara put her hand to her mouth, watching them carry past a tiny bleeding bundle. It was an unconscious little girl, her brightly-coloured robe wrapped around her like a dressing. The baby skin of her face was spattered with blood.

17

Through the cotton, Dara saw a foot protruding at an extraordinary angle from one calf. On the other side, if she was seeing right—and she couldn't even be sure she was—apart from a hanging piece of blood-drenched fabric, there seemed to be nothing.

'Jesus Christ.'

'How bad?' said Tom.

'Bad, bad...' muttered Miloš.

Dara's eyes shot full with tears and her throat seized. She felt like she was going to puke, or cry, until she remembered the little boy, who was following behind them, his cries hoarse and weak now, and breaking down into sobs. She took a deep breath and put her arms around his shoulders. Once the door of ambulance was closed, the boy covered his face with his hands and struggled as Dara tried to walk him away towards the truck.

'Tom, you drive!'

She managed to get the boy inside and when Tom started the engine, the boy rolled his head into her shoulder, choking with grief.

All she could do was hug him and murmur words she hoped might sound comforting. A roaring ball of energy five minutes beforehand, flailing and shouting all over the road, he was now just a skinny little kid in deep anguish.

As the ambulance pulled alongside, he clawed at the window, trying to get out.

'Easy, easy.' Dara held him back as she rolled down the window.

'She's stable now, we go to hospital.' Karel called over.

'Okay, Sergeant,' Dara said. 'See you there.'

18

The ambulance sped off down the desert road, and Tom pulled out after it. Dara looked at the boy. He had calmed down a little by now, as if in defeat. His face, streaked with tears and dust, bore an expression that no child should ever have.

'Dara,' she said, putting her hand on her chest. 'Me, Dah-ra. You?'

'Hassan.'

'Okay, Hassan. Okay. Hassan, where is your Mother, Father? Mama?'

He began to cry again, pointing down the road, in the direction they were going. As they pulled out he leaned into her, head against her rough army fatigues. He had one of those lean desert faces, high cheekbones, hair still in soft childish curls. His baggy cotton shorts were probably issued by some NGO, his T-shirt too, which bore the welkin-eyed duo of Leo and Kate mooning nobly into the middle distance with the Titanic hovering under them. Except that Leo and Kate were all spattered with blood.

After about ten minutes the boy gestured at the road ahead and said something, repeating it for emphasis. She nodded, let go the little hand she had been holding and sat back. He straightened up and faced out the window. After a half kilometre he pointed again as an IDP camp came into view.

The encampment was a small one, with about a dozen huts huddled around a main clearing. In the midday light the place looked baked and desolate, the sand littered with domestic debris. There were some traditional huts made up of palm leaves and wooden frames, but the rest were corrugated iron shacks, makeshift and unstable. It boasted the usual menagerie of goats, chickens and mangy dogs.

Before the truck had even stopped, the children were swelling into a pint-sized welcoming committee, their grins and cheeky stares tumbling up a little cloud of glee.

When the truck rolled to a halt, Hassan scrambled down and set off towards a tarpaulin-capped dwelling at the far end of the compound. She followed him as fast as she could, wading through the children, whose excitement turned to anxiety when the calm of the compound was shattered by a woman's scream. Wailing followed, and shouts, as adults emerged from other huts, running towards the commotion.

Dara ran with them, until she was in front of a wattles and recycled- metal shack. Kneeling in the sand was a woman about the same age as herself, who gripped the boy's arm tightly with one hand. She was shouting, sobbing, running her words together. An older woman was holding her. For the second time that day Dara felt completely helpless. No interpreter. The only thing she could think of to do was to offer the mother her hand. She was relieved when the woman took it.

From behind the hut, a man in an embroidered cotton skullcap appeared and stood listening to Hassan tell his story in a mixture of words and tears. The man was an older, tougher version of the boy and fired angry questions at his son.

Dara stood up to address the man. 'We'll take you to the hospital.'

He turned to her and glanced up and down her fatigues with mistrust.

'Il ospedale en Aban,' she added.

'Okay,' he looked directly at her. The tone said that even if he didn't speak English, he knew damn well she was not

Italian. She dropped her eyes, reminded that historically the Afar were a tribe of warriors, not Internally Displaced Persons.

As they waited for the parents, Dara looked at the villagers' faces. They were concerned, curious; some of the younger men looked angry. The children now looked frightened. The parents returned and they made their way back to the road accompanied by the group of villagers, who spoke in low voices as they walked.

Forty-four degrees, easy. Shit. She noted how Tom's shirt was soaked from collar to waist down the button seams and around the armpits, and she had to stop herself imagining her brains coming slowly to the boil inside her cranium. Beginning to feel a little dizzy, she breathed out as slowly as she could. Light dehydration, easily remedied. She was grateful her sunglasses hid her eyes, grateful she had arms and legs intact. Grateful she didn't have to speak.

Just before they got into the truck, Hassan tapped Dara on the arm and held out his hand. She took it in hers and he shook it solemnly, like an old man.

The mother cried in the back seat as they headed for Aban, her bright cotton veil draped over her face.

'She'll be alright, Missus,' Tom said. 'She'll be grand, don't worry.'

The father gazed silently at the road ahead. On the outskirts of the battle-broken town, the hospital came into view. Like most of the old Italian buildings, it could be seen from the distance, grandiose and completely alien among the palm trees, yet picture-postcard-placed beside the turquoise sea. With its marble columns and ornate balustrade, it had once been a jewel in the crown of the colonial administration.

It had been badly damaged by the bombs dropped on it during the battle for the port.

Tom pulled up in front of the hospital. The flight of steps going up to the main entrance had been partially destroyed and didn't look safe. Dara nodded at a sign on their left saying ENTRATA and they walked quickly around the side of the building and through a ground- level doorway.

Stepping inside the casualty department was like slipping through a crack in time. The long, low-ceilinged hall had institutional marble floors and its sombre green walls were lined with what must have been Soviet-era health posters. Everything was faded like a vintage snapshot. Dara approached the receptionist at the front desk.

'Good afternoon, I'm Lieutenant O'Neill from the Hibernian Peace Contingent, we are here with the parents of a little girl who stepped on a landmine.'

'Please wait,' the receptionist said, picking up the phone.

Families perched on rows of wooden benches or chairs, and those incapable of sitting lay on benches along the walls, groaning or suffering in silence. Down the back, smoking, sat a cluster of ex-combatants, most with amputated or half-amputated limbs. Their wooden crutches leaned on the benches beside them, and they still wore their revolutionary khakis. There were sick children everywhere — some crying and some lying immobile in their mothers' arms. Others were playing around on the floor. She noted several children with bad eye infections, others with swollen bellies.

'Commander Dara?' A young nurse in a crisp medical uniform emerged from a doorway to their right.

'Lieutenant.' She gently corrected, holding out her hand. The young woman took it in hers with a warm smile.

'I am Nazareth, I speak English. I will bring you to see Doctor Girma, the Hospital Chief.'

Nazareth continued to chat as they went up a polished wooden staircase.

'The Doctor will enjoy to meet you. He study in America.'

'Oh, what part?'

'Michigan. He come home to help his country after the war. He is nice man. Very sad.'

'Sad?'

In a small dispensary at the top of the stairs, a man in his early forties sat writing in a yellow legal pad at an almost empty Formica-topped desk. His smile didn't quite reach his eyes as he stood up to greet them.

'Welcome. I am very sorry that you are brought here on this terrible occasion.'

Sitting down again, he was framed by the window, with the sea in the distance dark blue against the horizon. With this back-light the room was surprisingly dark, and the only other furniture was a couple of almost bare medical cabinets. His face was grave as he addressed the parents first in Zohmean, and then spoke to Dara and Tom.

'Doctor Svenson — he is volunteering with us — is operating on the girl now.'

'Will she survive?' Dara asked.

'We will do our best, but, unfortunately, we have limited resources. Our supplies are extremely low. We have almost no Demerol, we need new surgical instruments, and we have very few vaccines. Sometimes there is no electrical power, as you know. We are the only hospital in the area, and there are more and more people every day.' He spoke without drama, only deep disquietude.

'Don't worry, Missus,' Tom said to the mother. 'It'll be grand. Your girl will be fine.'

'For Jesus' sake, Tom,' Dara snapped. 'Sorry, Doctor, you were saying?'

'Her recovery will depend on how long she lay out in the terrain, how much blood she has lost,' Doctor Girma replied.

'And long term?'

'Well, as I said, we have limited facilities.'

'You could try Minefree Planet,' Tom interrupted.

'Yes. If the government permits them access, they may help,' the Doctor said. 'But otherwise…'

Otherwise, she'll be one of those sad kids on crutches in postconflict zones the world over Dara reflected. 'Doctor, maybe we can do something in the Base to fundraise?'

Doctor Girma nodded. 'Thank you.'

'Do you mind if we do a whip around this evening for the family—' Tom said, 'unofficially, like?'

This time the smile reached the doctor's eyes, but it was almost one of bemusement. 'If you do, it would be very kind.'

'It's always worse when it's a kid,' Tom said, as they walked out of the office. He looked at her, waiting for a reaction. Dara said nothing. It was certainly the worst thing she had ever seen happen to a child.

At 15:00 hours Captain Neary crackled in over the hand-held, telling them to stay where they were as a gesture of support for the family. Instead of waiting in the Emergency Room, they were all seated in a small parlour overlooking a weed-choked garden. It was convent-like; a scrubbed-clean oilcloth covered the table and lace doilies lay under vases of plastic flowers on a sideboard. A girl brought in sugary black tea on a tray, and they drank it, sweating, but pretending not to.

Dara couldn't get Dr Girma's face out of her mind. He could have lived the dream in Michigan, but he came home to help his country. And he was sad. Such a simple word.

Nazareth did her best to ease conversation with her translating skills, but their exchanges were infrequent and politely strained. Dara felt they could have been in a waiting room in Beirut, Singapore or Galway Regional — anguished parents awaiting news in hospitals didn't really differ wherever they were.

'What age is your daughter?' Tom asked.

Nazareth translated. 'Five years old.'

Tom looked a bit taken aback. 'What's her name?'

'Selam,' the father answered, without raising his head.

'It meaning peace,' Nazareth added. 'Many girl babies give this name when the war ended.'

Tom was quiet for a minute, looked like he was about to say something, then appeared to clam up. He cleared his throat noisily. The parents glanced at him, surprised. Dara was even more surprised.

'I have a daughter her age, you know.' Tom said. 'Born at Easter, 1998.' Nazareth translated this without difficulty.

'My girl's name…' he said, 'is Saoirse.'

'Seer-sha?' Nazareth repeated. Dara spoke for Tom, trying to choose her words well.

'That is…it's a girl's name that's very similar to Selam's in our language,' Dara said. 'It means freedom.'

The father responded with a grave nod to this information. Nazareth translated his following question.

'He say, your country have war also?'

When Nazareth brought the parents to their daughter downstairs at eighteen hundred, Dara decided it was time to head back to the Base. Outside on the steps, cigarette in hand again, Tom was about to launch into conversation.

'Tom, why don't you head back in the truck, it's only a ten-minute walk.'

'But it's getting' dark, like…'

'I'll be grand. Just want to say a little prayer…' She nodded towards the hospital church, a little apart from the main building down a side road parallel to the highway. She knew that would shut him up.

'Right, so.' He looked somewhat incredulous. 'Take it handy, Lieutenant.'

'No worries, mate…' she said it in the Aussie drawl Tom was so fond of, getting a grin out of him as he headed for the truck.

'No wuckan furries!' he shouted back. 'No wuckers!'

The church was set back in a shady, overgrown garden with a rusting jeep abandoned under a tree. On it perched a large dark bird, apparently unperturbed by her presence. Dara felt a shiver, despite the heat. It struck her how savage and disturbing the twisted metal seemed, interrupting a place so naturally at peace. The multi-hued murals, still brilliant

26

against the walls despite the dusk, had been done by a local artist. Broad sprays of machine gun fire had punctured the haloes of several saints, but they remained on the wall, looking holy and wise regardless. From the base and around the corners of the walls, stains of black and dark green damp seeped up from the ground. A makeshift roof of corrugated iron looked newer than the stonework. She hesitated before stepping onto the path that led through the garden, but it looked well trodden and clear.

Over the entrance, what must have been a stained glass rose window was blocked up with metal panels, but the carved wooden doors were still intact, framing the entrance to the church like ancient sentinels. The side windows, with simple blue and yellow panes, were illuminated now from the west. As the stars slowly punched life into the darkening sky above her, she looked up at the painted Jesus that graced the bell tower. With his dark locks and big brown eyes, a robe of deep red and perfect black rubber revolutionary's sandals, he was different from the pale, lion-blond figure of her childhood.

Dara removed her boots in the women's entrance hall, and went inside. She didn't feel like an intruder here: maybe a bit out of place with her sweat-drenched fatigues and greasy ponytail, but the Madonnas, the gilded paintings and incensed air had a parish church's familiar air of sanctuary. She lit a candle at the Virgin's shrine and sat down on a straw mat beside her, drained. Soldier girl. Shit. The briefings hadn't fucking mentioned what happens to your heart. They didn't tell you that part at all.

That night in the base she slept fitfully, plagued with confused and horrific dreams about kids playing near minefields. She was at the door of an APC begging a little girl to come inside, agonising about whether to leave the cool safety of the vehicle or walk out across the sands and bring her back. She would wake up, lose the dream and turn over into another full of bloody children, ambulances that had disappeared, amputees staring from shadows and all palled with some ineffable horror to come.

She finally dragged herself upright and put Steve Earle on full blast through her headphones, making the bed, tidying her container, jumping around to the joyous, horror-chasin' twang of 'Guitar Town'. In her mind she was back five years earlier in Whelan's pub in Dublin, kicking around to some local band trying to make good. Feeling the crush of the dancers, music eclipsing everything. Rock 'n' roll. The bass beat through her heartache like a thump on the back from an old friend.

At dawn, she climbed up on the sandbags at the edge of the perimeter to watch the day breaking, the blinding gold of the sun soaring up out of the horizon and igniting the surface of the desert around the camp. A row of white armoured personnel carriers stood silhouetted against the sky, and she was somewhat renewed at the sheer beauty of it. Desert as Turner painting. With military hardware.

After that, she walked across the yard to the officer's mess and, to her disgust, saw her hands were shaking again. Only one thing required — well, at this hour anyway. A good strong cup of tea. She put two Barry's Red Label bags into the mug, filling it with boiling water from the Burco and squished them around well to ensure tea so strong you could trot a mouse on it. She remembered trying to explain this phrase to a Canadian military advisor two days previously without much success and smiled, until she caught sight of Tom, charging across the yard on a mission. She walked outside and sat down at a table, cup tight in one hand, the other in her pocket.

'Lieutenant, we're going back to the hospital, right?'

'Look, Tom, I don't think there's much more we can do.'

'It's Sunday, but ...'

'Yeah, look—we can't get involved, okay?'

'Bullshit. We were fuckin' asked to show solidarity. That's orders, isn't it?'

Dara glared at him. Bastard. He wouldn't talk like that to a male officer. She waited a beat.

'Lieutenant.'

'Okay.' She sighed. She knew it was what she wanted to do, yet part of her was dreading going back. 'Yeah. I'll need to do the incident report anyway. Might as well go today.'

'What about the whip-around?'

'Oh, shit.'

'Forgot that, didn't ye?' Tom said, taking out a scrunched-up brown paper bag from his pocket. Inside she saw a small roll of bills, dollars as well as local currency and some change.

'God, that's brilliant.'

'It'd take three months to go through UW officially.'

'Well done, Corporal.'

'Jayzis, we could go to Sharm El Shiekh for the weekend with this!' he said.

Dara laughed. 'Now there's an idea...'

Their jeep snaked along the potholed road, past the Martyr's cemetery and the war memorial. Past palm trees and dust and an indigo sea that people back in Ireland might dream of.

'Tom,' Dara said, 'I don't think we should be expecting any miracles, you know? I mean, the best we can hope for is to see her alive.' Tom just kept his eyes on the road and didn't answer.

At the hospital, they walked up a long, sweltering corridor to a small room on the first floor. But there were no miracles. A curved metal frame had been placed over her legs, raising the hospital sheets into a mound that hid the main damage. She was hooked up to two different drips, and deathly pale. The adult hospital bed was three times longer than her little body and made her look all the more vulnerable. Her mouth was half-open, a tiny rosebud lip split open on one side, and she was breathing loudly, faster than Dara would have expected.

The father stood up and made a momentary fuss of greeting Dara and Tom, but there were no smiles this time around. Tom coughed, almost embarrassed.

'Bambina...' he said, stuffing the brown paper bag into the man's hand. The father did not look inside, but felt the contents and gave a small nod of acknowledgment. Tom nodded back and they shook hands.

Then they resumed a quiet vigil. The mother, face framed by her brilliant red and yellow headscarf, looked shattered. She did not move, only keeping hold of her daughter's free hand on one side of the bed, the other all wired up. White bandaging on the child's forearms concealed the harm with sterile perfection, and her torso was also bandaged.

They had been there only a half-hour when Selam began to whimper now and then, turning her head from side to side or freezing momentarily as shivers pulsed through her whole body, baby teeth clenched and fingers curled into tiny balls of pain. The eyes shot back and forth and after a minute she fell back into her sedation. The first time it happened the father stood up, bewildered, and walked out to the corridor. Then he came back and sat down again, dropping his eyes to the floor; his own pain almost palpable. After it happened a few times, the mother began softly crying.

'Tom, get a nurse.'

Tom hurried out as Selam's agitation worsened. Dara watched her anxiously, thinking of the luxury of mere nightmares.

Nazareth arrived and gave Selam a syringe of Demerol, patting the hair matted with sweat. The mother's frown softened as she watched the child's body relax little by little. After a few minutes, Selam opened her eyes sleepily and smiled at them all. Her mother stroked the back of her fingers across her daughter's forehead, cooing and whispering to her. She smiled at her father and at Tom.

Dara was unable to hold back silent, stinging tears. She turned and stood to look out the window, feeling the heat already building up in the air outside. The worst thing she had ever seen happen to a child.

'How is she doing, Nazareth?' Tom asked.

'One leg gone, one not good,' she answered.

'Will you tell the parents we are very sorry about Selam?'

The mother smiled and then spoke urgently to Nazareth.

'She want to know if you can help Selam after she is out of hospital?'

'We'll try our best,' Dara answered, coming back to the bedside. 'We can inform the landmine project or see if Minefree Planet can assist with a prosthetic limb.' The mother didn't look convinced.

'Nazareth, I've been asked by my boss to write up a report,' Dara continued. 'When do you think I would be able to talk to Selam, and will you ask if that's okay?'

'Now is a good time to talk to her, she is comfortable now. I can translate,' Nazareth said. She spoke to Selam's father and he nodded.

Selam was smiling at a small toy that her mother was waving in the air at her eye level, and seemed, as the nurse said, to be at ease. She was not unwilling to describe what happened.

'She say she frightened she lose baby goat, she see goat running on the rocks and she think is okay to go there,' Nazareth said.

Dara wrote in the notes. Her mother stroked Selam's hair.

'There was a big bang — she remember flying.' She asked the girl another question. 'I think she remember nothing else.' For a few minutes, the only sound was Dara's pen scribbling and the ceiling fan overhead.

'Probably an M14 anti-personnel mine,' Tom said. 'They're all around here. Designed to take off a soldier's booted foot...'

Nazareth didn't translate this, as Selam had begun to speak again.

Her father dropped his head, putting the heels of his hands into his eyes.

'She say she sorry for be disobedient. Very sorry. She ask about the animal...' Nazareth's voice faltered.

'Selam, thank you,' Dara said through Nazareth. 'You're a good girl. The little goat is safe, don't worry. You didn't do anything bad. The bomb that hurt you is the bad thing.'

Suddenly Tom leaned in towards Nazareth, his clenched fists dug into the middle of his thighs, the knuckles white. There was an angry edge to his voice.

'Listen, will you ask her something for me? Ask her did she not see the warning signs—the red ones—they're up all along the road, in the local language even. Didn't she see them?'

Nazareth spoke very softly this time. Dara held her breath and the fan whirred. Its stream was tepid and sweat was beaded over the child's brow. It almost looked like she was going to drift back into sleep, but then she gave a response, short and simple.

Nazareth leaned back in her chair and looked at Tom, then lowered her eyes again.

'She can't read. She say she thought they were pretty pictures.'

And then Selam did drift back to sleep.

BLUE TARPAULIN

I am blue plastic, a simple thing. Mass produced, distributed in panic, witness to horror, immune to it. I have no voice, no sight. I have no bones, no arms, no brain, but I am the world's unlikely protector in the places it prefers to forget.

I am received into the shaking arms of widows, orphaned children; and with me comes a kind of hope beyond the comprehension of those who finance my manufacture.

My shelter comforts the homeless. I am a roof, a wall, a house.

Make me a frame and I will make you a dwelling for a family fleeing death and horror. Hand me out to all the displaced and I will make you forty million dwellings.

In bombed villages I make so many roofs that from overhead I look like a ruins-and-blue patchwork quilt. What a sorry bed to lie on.

I have travelled to the world's worst places — to squalid camps too long extant, and never-ending war zones.

I have no heart, no hands but sometimes I give more than those who have.

I am a stretcher for a bleeding mine victim. I am the

bed on which babies are born. I am the shroud in which the massacre victims are covered.

I collect rainwater to alleviate thirst. I envelop bags of grain to keep them dry. I protect medicines on trucks climbing mountain passes to plague-stricken outposts. From within my folds, the eyes of mothers watch for the big white water truck. Hoping it will be white, not warring green.

I am a simple thing, I have no love, I have no politics. I am all-seeing of man's brutal follies, although I have no eyes. I ask no recompense, I make no comment, I do so much.

I am blue plastic bearing a white symbol that sullies fast with desert dust and mountain muck, until its purity has faded to a shade somewhere between nightmare and desperation.

But my blueness stays — all around the world: desert, mountain, riverbank, plain. A humble, dirty, plastic blue, ubiquitous, necessary.

Sometimes, I am the most that can be done, under the circumstances.

THE BIGGEST LIAR

Bren stood under the canopy of the medical tent and pulled on his cigarette, trying to make sense of the day. The stench of disinfectant and death wafted from inside, but the overhead flap provided shade from the sun, still fierce despite the hour. Around his feet a trail of cigarette butts peppered the dust. He added one more and put his hands into his pockets.

In the middle distance, a line of women and children were queuing up to have bright plastic jerry cans filled with water from a big white United World tanker. He watched as kids shouted and messed around as kids do, staggering back into the tent city with full containers. The Indian soldiers were chatting with some young women at the top of the line, and despite himself, a smile lit up Bren's face as one raised the water hose in the air and briefly drenched the crowd, prompting squeals and laughter.

He would tell Ciara this story. The Indian peacekeepers bringing the water and the girls laughing. Life-affirming, as the Americans say. He'd be a good guest. He wouldn't tell her about the stick-insect toddler that had died at the back of the medical tent five minutes before, of the smell and the flies and the heaving sobs of the mother. The tears of the nurse. He could tell her about the school run by the ragged little man under the only tree for miles. That was how you made sense of it.

Tomorrow night in his sister's antiseptic Sutton kitchen he would be eating braised venison in a reduced claret *jus* with minted *petits pois* over a sweet potato mash. In between, somewhere, he would sleep.

It seemed cowardly to admit to this tiredness, but after over a year in-country, and the last four days on the border, he was tired. Too many whiteboards, he thought. Too many meetings and not enough talking to refugees. Not enough talking to people. *People.*

Moving from the stuffy office to the yard behind the admin containers that morning hadn't really helped, the sun was so intense that the small courtyard trapped the heat instead of providing shade. After the clinic visit, the visitors had been told to chill until sixteen hundred, when a chopper would bring them back to the capital. He figured he'd just walk around for an hour.

Refugee camp. Two simple words he'd heard on the news since childhood. But no amount of repetition could ever have made him understand what they actually meant, until he spent two days in one, interviewing the displaced and the disenfranchised, taking photos, getting a bad sunburn and mild food poisoning. The previous night he'd slept under a mosquito net in the staff compound. Around dawn, he'd awoken to the sounds of two field doctors making love quietly in a tent nearby. There was something oddly affecting about it.

Across the dried-out laneway, a boy was watching him. Hands at his sides, he was dressed in absurd clothing: a Benetton polo shirt and ragged chinos hanging off his skinny body like a bad joke. He stood with one foot an inch deep in a stream of shit. Or that's what it looked like. Channels of waste-water made their way everywhere around the camp, curling down between the tents, full of unknown filth. The kid didn't appear to mind. He held up an invisible camera and mimed taking a photo of Bren. Bren returned the favour with his Canon, prompting the boy to cross the lane and look at the view screen.

When a crowd of other kids milled around demanding photos too, the boy chased them away, or at least as far away as he could.

'I am Abel,' he said, shaking Bren's hand. The handshake was tight, confident.

'Bren.'

'Where you go?'

'For a walk.'

'I bring you — best photo.'

Abel was staring at him, waiting for an answer. It would be rude to refuse, Bren decided.

'Okay,' he told the boy. 'Lead on.'

Bren walked after him up the sandy field and the little crowd of children followed about three metres behind.

In the tent city, there were eighteen thousand people going about what had become their daily lives. UWHQ had left Nadhin camp until the last stop on the visit, to show the inspection party from Prague how it had degenerated since its emergency construction three years previously. How it now needed a massive new influx of funds, very fast. Not two words usually associated with Prague. Bren had been sent along as a representative of The Juno Project to write up the NGO's own report. Good job there was a guideline on what to cover, because otherwise, where would he start? The camp seemed to have no beginning and no end.

'Where you from?' Abel turned and asked him.

'Ireland.'

'My teacher from Ireland. I learn English.'

'Here?'

'Sudan.'

He realised that Abel was bringing him up one of the low hills that he had seen in the distance from the entrance buildings. It was hard going on foot in this heat. Slightly breathless, at the top of the slope, they stopped.

'Best photo,' Abel waved an arm at the view.

Bren looked out at the landscape below, his mouth opening as his eyes moved left to right and back again.

'Thanks, Abel,' he managed to say after a moment.

'Jesus…'

What they had seen up until then was only the camp's spillover. The main, older part of the camp stretched out across a ragged wasteland. For a moment every single thing was so sharply focussed it cut into him almost physically.

There was something here so out of control, a million whiteboard presentations could not convey the scale of it. Bren knew that his modest camera would definitely not capture it. A confused, bleached-out stain would fill the frame of the image and none of its power would translate. He took the photo anyway. Abel beamed.

They began their descent into the heart of Nadhin, walking past rows and rows of dwellings, some almost organic in their construction of stakes, grasses and refuse. Others were straightforward United World issue tents, white or blue canvas, rotted in parts, logo discoloured by the ubiquitous dust.

More again were of brown canvas, military-hued drapes that were faded and torn, The Juno Project's own plastic sheeting with its goatskin crest among them. The flaps of the tents were held down with ragged rope, the roofs slung over with large blue plastic tarpaulins and tied down on each side.

In front of the tents people were washing clothes, cooking rice, rocking babies — this went on and on as far as you could see. Outside one dwelling a woman in her fifties was weaving a multi-hued wicker basket, drawing strands of straw through and around tiny vertical shoots of wood, pressing down to make the sides of the basket solid. It was a thing of beauty. She looked up and shot him a smile, nodding her head. Her intricately plaited hair framed a gaunt face. He smiled back. Further on an old man was trying to adjust something on his tent. His solemn eyes gazed at Bren, as he paused in his task of trying to knot together two pieces of rope.

The man motioned for Bren and Abel to approach the tent. He spoke to Abel in a nasal, hoarse voice, showing him the material. The gnarled fingers that held the rope were tarnished with days-old muck, bones distorted from arthritis. There was a bitter smell of woodsmoke and sweat.

'He say look this bad tent — he house,' Abel translated. 'This ting — roof for family. Everyting broken.'

The old man handed Bren the worn rope. As Bren felt the rotting skein, a kind of sandy powder fell through his fingers. It probably wouldn't last much longer. Next month was rainy season, with its black sky deluges cropping each day into a few merciless hours, the destruction washing away roads and bridges, let alone canvas tents.

'I'm sorry,' Bren said to Abel. 'Please tell him I'll see if I can get him some better rope.'

The man responded to Abel with a quiet sigh.

'Okay. He say when?'

Good question. How the fuck would he get new rope? Raise a requisition? This was an old man without an address. The man leaned his head to one side, never taking his eyes off Bren.

Just then Bren's handset crackled. Lorenzo, fuck it.

'Juliet Papa 1 to Juliet Papa 3, over.'

'Juliet Papa 3, I read you, over,' said Bren, stepping back a few feet.

'What is your location, compañero, chopper ETA twelve minutes, over.'

'Okay, J1, there in ten, over.'

'Hope so, J3. Home leave tonight, yes?'

'Yes, over.'

'Walk fast. UW Air Ops don't wait. Over and out.'

He could not afford to miss this chopper. He turned to Abel. 'Okay, tell him I have to go now, I'm sorry.'

The old man was still looking at him, pleading his case as much as his pride would let him. Bren shook his head and looked directly at him. 'I promise. I will get some new rope for you.'

The man's eyes were doubtful. 'Thank you, Meester.'

41

Bren took off up the track then, Abel in pursuit, and after a few hundred metres a jeep with two local camp staff in it pulled alongside. He handed Abel the only thing he could think of—his pen—and repeated his thanks. Abel accepted it and drew back to the edge of the track, letting the hand holding the pen drop to his side, no longer smiling as the jeep pulled away.

'Abel, can you go down to the office tomorrow?' Bren shouted. 'I will send rope!' Abel didn't respond and after a few seconds disappeared in the dust raised by the vehicle as it hurtled down the track.

Bren leaned forward, holding on to the seat in front of him. 'Hey— do you work for camp admin?' he asked the driver.

'Yes.'

'There was an old man…the rope on his tent is broken. I promised to try and get him some new rope.'

'Write email, no problem.'

'No, that boy knows where he is. I need it sooner.'

'Soon? Today?'

'Tomorrow.'

The driver made a face. 'Have money?'

Bren sat back in the seat. Of course. He would need money. Bren had no money on him. Typical. All he had was a fucking ballpoint pen. To give to a boy with no shoes.

Kids were lined up all along the helipad fence and cheered at the white jeep as it stopped at the gate. He barely had time to haul himself inside the Mi8 before the flight officer drew up the metal steps and closed the door. He found a place on one of the bench seats running each side of the interior, between a quietly furious Lorenzo de Campo and a Scottish logistics officer.

He locked his safety belt as the blades warmed up into the deafening roar that signified enough power for take-off. Then he took out his iPod, put in his earphones and sank back against the porthole as Bowie joined the cacophony. Already, the location of the old man's tent was lost to him. An involuntary sigh escaped his lips and he closed his eyes. He felt like the biggest liar in the world.

Bren stared up at the lime-green, four digit blocks flapping on the screen that hung over the departures hall in Heathrow. Dubai, Milan, Paris, Istanbul, Stockholm — Dublin. Squinting under the lights, he slouched down the corridor to his gate.

On board this last plane of the journey, Bren pulled out his laptop to watch the end of a movie. It seemed to fast-forward in bursts against his will, but it was only him dozing off every few minutes. A swill of sour Egyptian coffee played fisticuffs in his gut with a block of gluten formerly known as German toast. He never thought he'd be grateful for Erinair. Yet here he was, in a calm, air-conditioned environment, with a home to go to and a sound pair of shoes that kept out the scorpions and the broken glass. He was on a safe aircraft that had a real seat and no groaning Medevac cases in it. The toilet worked. The quasi-Celtic scrolls that made up the pattern on the seatback in front of him looked extravagant, almost too pretty for their purpose. It would be nice to see Ciara. Maybe.

The air hostess woke him to straighten up his seat as they were coming into land. Glancing out the window, he was momentarily startled, expecting the dusty brown swathe of a desert landing strip. Peering through the rain, a sodden grey-greenness was visible on each side of the runway. He felt a brief sense of relief, a kind of gratitude that it was still there, wet and grey: home.

His sister stood just beyond the barrier, all red nails and tailored suit, new boyfriend in tow. Kev. In finance. Or that's Finance to you, mate. Way too fancy glasses for a straight man, but a solid Northside accent that somewhat redeemed him. Ciara was effusive, charged with her usual Celtic Tiger verve.

'So great to see you…brilliant. But look at the state of you, poor muppet. You're in bits! Are you starving?'

'I'm grand.'

'I'm going to make a full Irish for you, okay?'

'I'm not really that hungry, Ciara…'

'We'll stop in at Valumart on the way home, to pick up some stuff, and then you can rest up. I have the spare room all ready. It's totally IKEA, you'll be nice and cosy.'

He watched the landscape through the tinted windows of Ciara's new Land Rover as they drove across North County Dublin and soon its steady blur began to make him sleepy again. He closed his eyes a moment, half-listening to Ciara going about her new house, and her job, and other stuff he wasn't really taking in.

'And what about yourself, anyway? Things going well?' 'Bren?'

He jumped, realising she'd just addressed him directly. 'Ehm, yeah...'

'Well, we're dying to hear what you've been up to over there. Later anyway, when you've had a rest.'

'Sure.'

He smiled at her and lay back against the seat again. At a traffic light, he caught her watching him in the rear-view mirror with some concern. His eyes were closing and opening beyond his control. He knew he didn't look well, not what she'd expected. Maybe he shouldn't have kept the e-mails quite so upbeat, full of the wonders of Africa and the great work they were all doing. A little reality would have been more honest.

Ciara veered left off the motorway down a curve, straight into a mammoth shopping centre.

'You stay here, now, Bren. We won't be a minute...'

Bren sat in the luxury of the back seat and touched the fragrant, fawn-coloured leather, the Alanis Morissette irony of it pure and almost funny. The last Land Rover he'd been in had a NO GUNS sign on the window, holes in the seats and blood on the floor.

Opening the door, he breathed in the cool air. He could smell the sea off in the distance. You never knew how much you missed the sea until you lived in a desert. The rain and sea had a damp, plain smell, so utterly different from the richness, say, of Senara's marketplace, with the sacks full of spices, the heat and cigarettes, even the donkey shit—and the arguing scent of fruits rotting and fresh all at once.

Stop it, he told himself. Stop switching worlds. He was here now and Ciara was going out of her way to be nice to him. He had to stop acting the zombie.

His feet felt strangely pampered as he walked across the smooth surface of the car park. It was new, perfectly finished, marked with gleaming white lines, like a slick piece of advertising.

Standing inside the doorway of Valumart, he gazed up at the high, vaulted rafters, and then from side to side. It was like a cathedral, the arches of the ceilings towering over the shoppers as they traipsed around the aisles, performing the ritual of choice. He felt small, humbled in all this abundance. To his right was the most astonishing selection of fresh vegetables in long, chilled cabinets.

'Wow! Basil. Coriander!'

'So?' Kev had spotted him from the organic counter.

'We tried to grow coriander in the patio of the Juno compound, but it always died,' Bren told him. 'Hey, avocado. And look at the nuclear broccoli!'

'Are you taking the piss, Bren?' Ciara coasted up behind them, amused.

'Can we buy some broccoli?' he asked.

'For breakfast?'

'What, so there's no vegetables in Zohmea then? Is that what you're trying to tell us?' Kev asked.

'Ehm...' Bren thought about how to answer him. Simply, no. There are not a lot of fresh vegetables in Zohmea. One of the Hindu volunteers had lost two stone in a field station along the border and broccoli cost ten dollars a head in the capital. He decided to leave it out.

Moving away towards the interior of the supermarket, he found himself blinking at the sheer volume and variety of goods. Aisle after aisle, shelf upon shelf, packet after packet. Rice, soups, eggs, biscuits for dogs.

One lane offered shampoos catering to all manner of hair requirements in all fragrances, from mango to juniper to soothing sea salts for essential repair. He picked up one that guaranteed to moisten those dry ends in less than ten days and thought of the traumatised child he had seen in the camp whose hair had copper-blonde split ends. No shampoo in existence could fix them, since they were signs of malnutrition, not sun damage.

Then, in Household, he saw a display of fifty-metre bundles of old-fashioned clothes lines, on special offer for €14.99. Such an easy purchase. He picked one up, ran the strong orange chord between his fingers. Something inside of him broke. He swallowed and clenched his teeth. Shit. He had to get real and lighten up. He was home now, and it wasn't like he'd never been in a supermarket before. He decided to find Ciara again. She'd sort him.

As he walked back through the store, flanked on both sides now by white fridges, he stopped again at a wall of soft drinks. He stared, and then began to count the different kinds of orange juice. Smooth, with bits, without bits, fortified with calcium, Vitamin C, from concentrate, freshly-squeezed, organic...

Ciara spotted him, her trolley laden with items that she thought might tempt Bren, whose main problem, she'd decided, was fairly drastic weight loss.

'Fancy anything there, Bren?'

'They have seventeen different kinds of orange juice.'

'Hey,' Kev said, coming up behind Ciara. 'We'd better get yah home, Bren, before you lose it altogether.'

'Shut up, Kev. Brendan, what's wrong, love?'

Bren glared at Kev, then backed away. He needed fresh air. He started to make for the exit, but there were suddenly way too many people, swilling around him, talking into white wires, trolley-filling. Everywhere he turned, things appeared surreal, or hyper-real, he didn't know. Maybe just bloody unfair.

By the time Ciara caught up with him, in the space between the bargain South African wines and the cash registers, Bren was down on one knee under the fluorescent lights of Valumart, face fallen into one hand. In the other hand, he clutched a twist of gaudy nylon rope. What on earth was he doing with that?

She flushed when she became aware of shoppers in the checkout queue staring at this random man whose pants were frayed at the back down near the heels, the fabric slightly faded. Whose jacket hung too large on his frame. Then she saw how the sweep of dark hair over his eyes was feathered with slim hints of grey, and understood that this was her brother, crumpled into a pile of grief in front of her. For a moment, she was almost overcome herself. She took a breath and hunkered down beside him, balancing on her work heels.

'What's wrong, Bren, what is it?'

Bren didn't answer.

'Are you alright? Tell me. Are you sick?'

'No, I'm fucking well.'

'What is it then?'

'Seventeen. Seventeen different kinds.'

Ciara put her hand on his shoulder and he could smell her Japanese perfume. Maybe he should tell her about the kid that died in the medical tent after all.

'Okay, Bren. You're exhausted, I can see it.'

'So much *stuff...*'

'Listen, you take the car keys, we'll finish up here and we'll be out in a few minutes, okay?'

Bren took the keys from her and got to his feet. His head was pulsing, his eyes burning. He jumped when the disembodied voice over the exit doors thanked him for shopping at Valumart. For a moment he hesitated, as if there was something he needed to do. Then he continued to the car park, clutching the gaudy nylon rope in his hand.

BLOOD AND BONE

Philippe, bleary from the night before, did a double take as he paid for his aspirin and cigarettes. The image that took up four front-page columns of the *International Weekly Examiner* was surely his, displayed across two shelves in the Addis Hilton gift shop. He walked over to the news rack, grinning. Definitely his photo, one he was sure they wouldn't use, but he'd fired it off to the agency anyway.

It was a simple shot, an instinctive click of the button as they were running for the chopper to get out of that awful place, whatsit – Speranza – a horror camp on the Sudan/ Ethiopia border. Thirty thousand lost souls, no running water and a skeleton detail of overworked aid staff losing their minds. She had been coming towards him up the road. He saw something; just something. Felt that visceral pull that dared him not to. Her height, her bearing, a certain majesty. He hardly saw the face but saw the shot. Stopped like a freight train in full throttle. Lift camera. Focus every muscle. Focus camera. Click.

He'd sent it more or less raw from camera; it hadn't even needed Photoshopping. It went along with a bunch of much more dramatic images – standard issue carnage maybe, but quality work. They'd reached a village just after a battle and there was one of a soldier on fire laying across a pile of washing, children's clothes smouldering around him. But they'd used the one of this tall girl instead.

A French couple by the card stand had just bought the paper. They were young; newly-weds, or maybe one of those couples stopping in Addis to pick up an adopted baby. The wife stared at the woman's face. Her eyebrows contorted and her lips rose up in the middle into a thin tight shape. She dropped her head and began to walk towards the lobby, all the while reading the adjoining feature. The husband followed.

Phil picked up an Examiner and checked the bi-line: NEUFOTO/P. VASQUEZ.

Yes. He looked at his cover girl. Finally, real international exposure. Despite his headache he couldn't help smiling. His phone upstairs must be full of messages by now. And tweets. Tweet tweet tweet.

He scanned the story. 'Survivors arrive in Speranza Refugee Base.' She'd been one of a straggle of people dragging up the dusty trail towards the camp gate. According to the report they were fleeing a rebel raid across the border where an estimated thirty community members had been killed. Those who had made it out had just reached Speranza as Phil's chopper was howling to take off from the helipad.

He decided to leave the phone upstairs and headed for the pool bar to celebrate. He ordered a St George. Finding an empty deck chair, he leaned back against a tufty blue towel drinking the beer as hair of the dog, a little too fast. Front page. Bringing the Examiner up between his face and the sky, he read the report.

> *Villagers were dragged out of their huts and subjected to beatings, torture and summary executions. Survivors reported that further atrocities included infanticide, rape and abduction.*

More of the same. If the earth is a woman like they say, she must have a broken heart for South Sudan. They even won their independence — the newest country in Africa — only to go back fighting, this time South against South. How fucking sad was that.

'Sir? Sir? Would you like a menu?'

He opened his eyes and shut them again quickly. Jesus, his cover girl was in front of him carrying a tray and wearing a Hilton waitress's uniform. He got up on one elbow.

'Excuse me?'

'Would you like to order something to eat, Meester Phil?'

Sitting up, he was relieved to see that it was pretty Yodit from Mekele and not the refugee woman. She sounded most persuasive, almost like a big sister. He should be so lucky. Well fair enough, he'd been knocking back the beers now for several hours; she was right. He'd better eat something. He ordered a burger and a Bati, for a change.

'Salad?'

'God no, Yodit. Fries please.'

It was pleasant here beside the pool but he couldn't stop looking at the newspaper. She kept drawing him in, as if it were personal. If she was walking so determinedly into Speranza Camp, the biggest hellhole in the region, what kind of hell had she come from? He read the story again.

> *One female refugee told this reporter, 'I have lost my husband; two of my children, my parents. They burned down our houses. My cousin was disgraced in front of the whole village. She died afterwards—and they took the boys away to be soldiers…'*

Later he spotted Duncan Williamson from *The Times* across the lawn and waved. Dunc sat down beside him.

'Congrats on the front page of *The Examiner*, Phil. That was some shot.'

'Oh yeah?'

'Who is she? Did you get to talk to her?'

'No.'

'God, that's a shame.'

'Took it on the fly. Had better action stuff from earlier but they ran with that one.'

'I can see why. Look at those eyes. They don't need a report.'

'Yeah?'

'You should lay off those cigarettes, Phil.' Dunc nodded at the garden table beside them, where an ashtray was dwarfed by a small forest of empty St George and Bati bottles.

'Party over on Bole tonight by the way,' Duncan said as he got up to go back to his room. 'Just near Aladdin. I'll be going over around nine…'

Philippe slipped into the soothing water of the pool, watching the steam evaporate into the early night sky. He dog-paddled without much effort towards the warmer water in the middle where the air smelled of sulphur over the natural spring below. It was supposed to have healing properties. Every time he thought of her—because now she was in his head—she became more solid, her eyes more wounded; that tiny exposure of skin on her right shoulder and down her arm became more vulnerable, just soft human skin. A person of blood and bone.

He headed back to his room for a shower and requested bottled water ice and peanuts so he could have a nip of his duty-free Jameson in the fridge.

He still hadn't opened the computer and the phone battery was dead. He knew he should be checking emails. He should be going through his recent shots to check for more he could send on to Paris, but he opted instead for a plan to grab a flea-dancehall taxi to the party near Aladdin and maybe one of those NGO girls, what the hell.

He brought his whiskey out on the balcony to get a start on the night. Sometimes you could be just wrong. Like that photo he'd got in Mog in 2005. He'd been sure it was a runner. A staggering, brutal shot of a dead mother and a hungry baby, perfect in its juxtaposition of evil and innocence. The Mogadishu rubble piled up around them, you could see debris around the mother's corpse as she lay on the street, black smoke clouded the top of the frame and a pool of oil aflame just feet away. The baby's tiny bloodied hand reached towards its mother's breast. Her torso was scattered with crumbs of cement and metal shards and the large piece of shrapnel that had just decapitated her lay behind her blurred body.

He'd thought it the best shot he'd ever taken at the time and Donovan's response from Berlin was incredibly annoying. 'It's not always about the spatter, Philippe...'

He knew that of late he'd been going after the hard core. Where else was there to go? *The Horror of War*. But he'd been photographing the dead and the dead couldn't always tell their stories with their eyes closed.

Her story was right there and she was alive. He picked up the paper yet again. She commanded the front page with her pain. Behind her somewhere in the clouded trees was the truth. Whatever the fuck that was, the devil only knew. And she was walking straight, looking right into the lens, wounded and fierce and dignified all at the same time – how was that. That was the word maybe: dignity. There wasn't a lot of it in his work, but wasn't that the point? Sometimes he would get back from the field and one photo out of a hundred would have him wound up like this, but why was she his first front page? Like she was negating all that went before.

The live music down in the terrace café had begun to play now and he pictured the tourists shuffling around the space in front of the band. He should head downstairs and get a cab to that party. It would be in full swing by now. He thought about it a bit then ordered a chicken curry from room service. Bottle of that crap South African wine. No side salad.

Much later, still on the balcony, he spill-slopped another measure of whiskey into his glass and stared into the pool eight floors down, a perfect turquoise cross in a manicured lawn edged with neat rows of white deck chairs and pretty little palm-covered huts. Strange that he'd never noticed that it was in the shape of a cross. The two newly-weds from this morning were cuddling at its edge, lit up from beneath as if by magic. They were smiling and kissing, oblivious and the muted sounds of sex-soft laughter reached him on the air. The wife had been moved at Phil's photo. She'd seen the woman and he had not.

He tried to remember the way he had looked at the first photos he'd taken in the field almost ten years before. A scene on a Khartoum-bound Antonov came to mind—him sitting in that war-movie hold, stinking soldiers, grubby white-shirted advisors and miscellaneous trauma-heads filling the bucket seats along each wall. Huddled into the canvas and rope weeping like a fool, as the people he had photographed slid image by image across the tiny screen of his Nikon in the gloom, digital ghosts. And after all of that, this. The media was nastier than ever these days and yet she was haunting the whole world with just her eyes.

He went into the bathroom to wash his face. Leaning over the basin he let his wrists luxuriate in the flow of clean water that gushed into the porcelain and then splashed it up over his neck and forehead and eyes. He raised his head to look in the mirror, saw a train wreck, eyes bloodshot, puffy bags below them. That nasty, dull ache was beginning at the back of his neck. He'd wanted to sleep around 2am, but he'd just kept drinking. Whatever the reason. No reason.

Whatever ...

It would be dawn soon and dawn at the Hilton would

be safe and solid and beautiful. The sun would make a picture postcard scene of the hotel garden, orange sky above illuminating the palm trees between the Mosque and the Coptic Church, the call to prayer would sound and petals of light would shimmer across the water. Another new day in a haven not so very far at all from a variety of hells ...

There was one day left now until his next assignment in Chad, with the *Irish Times* stringer. Darfur was reaching saturation point and they wanted coverage of the Hibernian contingent working hard for peace, outside their comfort zone. He bet those boys were sorry they'd left Tipperary by now alright.

He walked back across the room to the balcony looking for his glass, tripping over his camera bag half-way. Fuck! He stood up again and kicked the bag back, then slung off his shoes, letting his toes enjoy the biscuit-coloured pile of the carpet for a moment. Time for bed. At the window, he could see the sky brightening over the shanty town beyond the hotel walls and he knocked back the last of the Jameson from the bottle before he drew the curtains. By eleven he'd need to get on to the office, so he plugged the phone in to charge on the desk, volume off.

Then he turned off the lights and flopped back on the silken bedspread closing his eyes, still dressed. He would sleep now, for a few hours. Finally. He would sleep heavily at first and then restlessly and then he'd wake up feeling like shit, but not just due to a hangover. He knew that she would be waiting for him somewhere in there, down inside his drunken sleep, the tall girl from South Sudan.

THE PACKAGE MAN

Flowers. A sea of them filled the square and she stood in the middle of it with the refrain of a song in her head: even the sky above Paris is in love with the Île Saint Louis. Eventually, Tahmina would return to this city to live happily ever after. That was the plan anyway. The chill in the air boded a tough winter, but she was escaping back to Africa, like an eager swallow. She crossed the river over the bridge at Nôtre Dame, still in good time to post her cards before catching the train to Charles de Gaulle.

On the square in front of the Hôtel de Ville pigeons puttered around her feet as she glanced up at the imposing stone façade, tinged gold in the evening light. Inside the post-office on the ground floor, there was a line going the full length of the place for stamps and express letters. She sighed, gauging the length of the queue and how long it would take to get through it. A long time. The line moved with painful slowness; only one of the hatches was open. The man in front of her smelled of garlic and cooking oil and the man behind her had been staring at her unflinchingly since he came in. She turned and glared back. Behind him was a tall African man in a grey suit, wearing glasses, followed by a prim elderly woman in pink lipstick and a blue woolly coat.

There was another delay at the hatch ahead, and by the time she reached third from the top, she had been waiting fifteen minutes. She glanced at her watch, calculating how long it would take her to pick up her bag from the hotel and get to the RER at Châtelet. As the man in front of her tried to hand a small package in to the clerk, she feared she'd be waiting fifteen more.

'Monsieur, postal services to Cambodian refugee camps are cancelled, since last month. As they are to Gabon, Mozambique and Syria. No more. Finished.'

'Is going to Thailand, Madame.' He spoke softly, with a pronounced South East Asian accent.

'No, no. Services cancelled. New rule, sorry. Next...'

The man paused, gave a nod of his head and began to speak again. The clerk squinted at him, lips down-curled as if she had just taken a bite of lemon.

'Monsieur, I cannot take that parcel. Now will there be anything else?'

Tahmina had moved around slightly so that she could see the man. She met him daily in her work, same status, different war. He was a fairly recent arrival, she thought, and struggling. He was painfully skinny, his shoes were falling apart and he wore a synthetic navy suit jacket with very wide lapels, and no tie. He looked down at the package in his small, fine hands, and began to explain again.

'This package is going to Thailand.'

'What? I can't understand what you're saying. Speak up.'

'Is going to Thailand, not Cambodia. Near border only.'

59

He appeared to be addressing the woman politely, but Tahmina recognised a grave, concentrated anger somewhere in his tone as he spoke. Carefully camouflaged.

'What is he saying, for God's sake? I haven't got all day.'

'I have sent things before.' The man didn't take his eyes off her, and maintained a pleasant expression, despite her rudeness.

'Move along, Monsieur! Move along! You aren't the only person in line here.'

The man didn't move. His resentment had ebbed and he lowered his eyes. His hands had begun to tremble, and he had a very slight twitch that, while almost unnoticeable before, had now become quite pronounced. This struck Tahmina with unexpected force. It was something she'd seen all her life, on the face of a different refugee, in times of stress. For just the briefest of moments he was her father.

She turned to face the man. 'Ko thod khâ...' Wrong language, of course, but it was a gesture. She said quietly, 'It is a new regulation, Monsieur.'

A glimmer of anger flared up in his eyes.

'Mademoiselle,' the clerk turned on her. 'This is none of your business, can you also move along!'

'They are not delivering packages to the Refugee Camps anymore at all,' Tahmina continued. 'They have stopped the service. Even though they are in Thailand, it is because they are camps. It's political. The Thai authorities won't deliver. See?'

She pointed at a printed sign taped to the glass at eye level, but he didn't look. His eyes lowered under a frown as if he were locking down.

'What's your plan, Mademoiselle?' The clerk snapped. 'To teach him French?' This got a laugh down the line.

'The gentleman was probably educated in French, Madame.'

'Oh, really? Well, he doesn't seem at all educated to me.'

Suddenly the tall African man behind them pushed past her to the front, and hissed through the hatch bars in a barely controlled anger.

'Madame—how dare you treat a person like this? Is it part of your job description to be a bitch?'

The woman behind the partition stood up and moved back a step.

'Get out! You have no right to talk to me like that.'

'Rights? You are talking about rights? You and your National Front bastards! Who gave you the right to treat a man like this?'

Tahmina could hear shuffling and sighs behind her.

'This man approaches you in good faith, for an honest reason…'

The African voice, in its rich, precise French, was rising at each phrase. 'And he addresses you with perfect civility. Then you treat him like a dog?'

The Asian man was staring at this unexpected defender with an expression that could have been disdain or admiration, almost disbelief.

'He's mad!' the clerk screamed.

Right on cue, the elderly lady in the woolly coat bleated, 'If you dislike us French so much, Monsieur, why don't you go back where you came from?'

The man with the parcel suddenly turned and touched

Tahmina's arm. In broken American English he said, 'Say him is okay. Is never mind.'

'Not okay!' the African shouted now, in English. He addressed the clerk again 'Ça va pas, non? You should apologise to this man.'

When a uniformed employee emerged from behind the counter and announced the police had been called, the African turned on his heel and walked purposefully towards the door, followed by the Asian man. Tahmina hesitated for a moment, then stuck the postcards in her pocket and went after them.

Outside, the African man disappeared down the steps of the Metro station on Rue Rivoli. Tahmina found herself falling into a hurried step beside the package man, who had started off southwards across the plaza. When a police siren sounded in the distance, they instinctually walked faster until they got to a café on the corner and sat down together at a table on the terrace, facing the quay.

She thought of the fine line between tragedy and farce and shook her head. He responded with a tentative smile, finally relaxing his death-grip on the parcel. They sat for a minute to get their breath back, just two figures on the crowded quay. A waiter in his shirtsleeves appeared, shivering.

'Bonsoir.'

'Bonsoir,' they answered in unison. Then they laughed. The waiter gave them a curious look as they got up and crossed the street, stopping again beside the river. Behind them the café was illuminated, with people at the window tables looking cosy and ignoring the view of the Pont d'Arcole and the darkening Seine. Tahmina shuffled a little, refrained from looking at her watch. She would have to take the opposite direction to go back to the hotel. There was nothing to say at all, really, and yet she was loathe to take her leave.

The man gave a short laugh, as if this was the way he started any sentence. 'Is okay now?'

'I think so.' Tahmina smiled back. 'I'm sorry about the parcel. I lived in a refugee camp once, I know what it's like to have family still in danger.'

The man looked at her quietly for a moment, as if he were about to start a conversation. But Tahmina looked at her watch without thinking and he said quickly, 'Maybe service come back again. To the camps.'

'I hope so.' Looking up, her eyes met an intense, opaque expression and she glanced away again across the river. 'It's cold, now the sun's gone down,' she said.

This time he did not smile. 'Cold here all the time.'

THE THOUSAND MILE RULE

Joni Mitchell played out the car window and into the sky as the road led them across arid plains towards the sea. It was good to be away from headquarters, with its giant white carpet of vehicles in the compound, its guards and badges and endless forms. There was still freedom of movement between the capital and the coast, so they had taken the chance to travel while they could. For the moment they were in a back-together-again glow. As he drove, Conrad's free hand rested lightly along Dara's thighs, she stroked the curve of his neck. The road carved its way down from the high plateau through Close Encounters mountains and jagged ridges, then rolling hills with a million hairpin bends, to flatten out gently as it approached the coast.

They'd spent the previous night in Oforo in the worst hotel ever, a sort of East-African David Lynch special. Once a lush desert oasis boasting Roman-style baths on a natural spring, the village had bustled with coffee houses, a small cinema and the Hotel Classico, said to have been a secret rendezvous for Italian movie stars. By the turn of the millennium, whatever had made it an oasis had long since dried up. Rusting army jeeps lay abandoned in the ruins of the old baths and it had become a run down pit stop on the post-conflict tourist trail. Sad rooms around the back housed women who serviced some of the travellers, mostly military. In the Classico's foyer, purple-hued photos of Sofia Loren and Marcello Mastroianni smiled forever sixties. The room came complete with bedbugs and a spectacular lizard in the corner, a natural mosquito repellent, but its real charm was a small stained-glass window facing east.

In the morning, dawn light danced through it, crazy as a shell-shocked butterfly around the walls of the already-warm room, while they tumbled hair and limb in the fragile bed. And those were the last colours she remembered before the brightening highway brought them out into the sandy terrain.

Instead of the dodgy hotel breakfast, they ate some day-old base camp croissants that they'd found in the glove compartment. Croissants and bananas, with coffee that they'd got the hotel owner's grandson to pour into a flask before they left. Not bad at all.

'You know, it would be nice to just come here some time and hang out,' Conrad said.

'Here?'

'Well, via Zanzibar maybe. We could spend a few days in a nice hotel there first. Some time when we don't have to be anywhere.'

'Some time when the two armies are all best buddies again?'

'Yeah,' he thought for a minute. 'Well, maybe not.'

'On the other hand, don't forget what our great Mission Commander said at the last press conference!'

'Which was?'

'That the peace process is on track and that all UW Staff and military peacekeepers are expected to be out of here by Spring.'

'Isn't that what he said last year?'

'It's what he says every year.'

After a while, they stopped the car. He stood at the edge of the tarmac, peeing insolently across the terrain, ponytail a China ink stroke down his back. She went around to the back of the 4Runner, hoping that a truck or jeep wouldn't pass by on the road and catch her, bare bum to the wind.

She joined him a few feet from the edge of the blacktop, following his gaze.

'Pretty bad, isn't it?' he said.

'What?'

'That. Out there. Did you look?'

She looked. Some rotting tanks in the distance, some debris, the usual twisted metal, scattered.

'Look again. Look close.'

She looked again, saw something very strange and took two steps forward to try and get a better view. Conrad snatched her elbow and pulled her backwards, hurting her arm.

'Hey!' she shrieked, twisting out of his grip.

'NEVER go off the road!' he roared.

'Okay! I know.' She bit her lip, shocked she'd forgotten the rule.

'Never!'

He stormed back to the vehicle and got in, slamming the door.

She remained where she was. She was shaking. This was

nothing to do with the road, of course. They were both over-reacting. She considered their situation: classic love triangle. Bull fucking shit. She stood there rubbing her arm, letting it sink in again, she needed a few moments.

The previous morning at 09:00 hours she'd been pretty sure she was the woman in his life. Then in two seconds flat she'd become the *other* woman. Touché. She breathed in and out slowly. The desert, like the sea, was a calming thing. Yet there was definitely something odd about this place.

She sought out the puzzle that had originally caught her eye. It was a slim white object that protruded from a piece of faded material on the ground. A pair of dried-out boots lay some metres away. She swallowed. The gleaming object suddenly came into focus as a human forearm. Just beside it, a skull was embedded half way into the sand. The piece of fabric was a soldier's fatigues, now covering his remains, and then his boots. Still there, right where he'd fallen.

Just ten feet away, another pile of fabric half covered by sand metamorphosed into a separate human form long deceased, yet still weirdly intact. She raised her eyes and scanned the desert, recognising more of the same without respite.

This was the battlefield that Tom had told her about on the Base the other morning. Hundreds of corpses, without even a prayer said over them to send them to rest. One soldier had been found by the Recce team leaned up against a rock, a small water canteen on the sand beside the skeleton. He'd sat there, had time to drink the last of his water... The scene blurred as her eyes filled with unlikely tears. She waited on the safety of the demined road, humbled, until the emotion passed.

She looked back at the car, where Conrad was staring at her from behind the wheel. He'd put his sunglasses on, so she couldn't see his eyes, but he was not happy. He looked tired. Handsome tired, of course. Treacherous handsome bastard tired. She had been warned about mission romances before leaving HQ, so there was no-one but herself to blame. Resolution would be a simple matter: take it or bloody leave it. Their illicit games paled to insignificance in the reality of this charnel house. Carrying on like they were in this place, she thought, it wasn't right. She got back in the car, quiet now.

'You hadn't seen that before, huh?' He said it without looking at her. 'Only the roads around here have been cleared, not the land. Too many mines out there still for them to go in and get the bodies.'

'How come they're all still there like that?'

'Desert bakes 'em. And the clothes. They're sort of mummified by the dryness and the sun.'

He leaned over and kissed her. 'Cheer up, mate. Buy you a beer in Baia, okay?'

'No worries, mate,' she conceded.

'Listen, Dara,' he said. 'This place is haunted. But we're alive, eh?'

She nodded and they moved on. Outside now, the volcanic plains never seemed to vary, only cloud shadows shape-changing now and then, curiously ephemeral on such a timeless expanse. She watched the sky instead, catching sight of an extraordinary bird overhead, dark head and broad white wings with dark tips, like an Audrey Hepburn hat. Four seconds of beauty and it was gone.

'So tell me a story,' she said.

'Okay. Boxing Day, 1999, Costaverde. UW is there to monitor the elections.'

'Yeah?'

'There's a convoy five million metres up the Sierra Madre.'

'Cold.'

'It's midnight too. Freeze your fucking balls off.'

'Got it.'

'You know Marina, from Comms?'

'Blonde Bosnian girl?'

He clicked his tongue and looked at her, grinning. 'Croatian.'

'Ah, right!'

'She's in a team whose vehicle runs out of petrol. Fuck! But hey — she finds a can in the back of another 4Runner, scoots back and pours it into their empty tank, so happy she's found fuel.'

'Except it was anti-freeze.'

Conrad bellowed with laughter. 'Shit, you heard it already.'

'I heard it was a military observer from Shandong Province.'

Conrad bellowed again.

'Right. Here's a Chas Bruen story then.'

'Now you're talking.'

'Iraq, 2002. In one of those God-awful desert forts where UW dumped our lot to demine hell on earth. Saddam used them as prisons.'

'Jesus.'

'You don't know the half of it. Rats, crappy generators,

radios that didn't work… And UW had reclassified them as *field offices*. So, one day they chopper up an Admin Officer from Baghdad to do a quarterly sitrep, right? Dave's mad as hell after three months of administrative bullshit and doesn't fancy entertaining a bureaucrat, so he gets a couple of the local staff to dress up as Mukhabarat.'

'Saddam's…'

'Secret Service, yeah.' Conrad grinned. 'So the plonker's just arrived, and he's in Chas's office enjoying his tea and bickies when they burst in, hold everybody up at gunpoint, pretend to kick the shit out of Chas and drag him off, screaming. This guy's pissing himself. Then they come back and haul him out, sling him into one of the cells in the keep.'

'That's savage!'

'That's fucking brilliant. Except that then the boys were so pleased with themselves they set to drinking a few beers out back after sunset and *forgot* about him…'

Dara clapped and threw her head back and when it came down again there was a tear of mirth running down her cheek. Shit, she thought. Every time she'd persuaded herself what a prick he was, Conrad disarmed her again. Every fucking time.

'Well,' she said. 'You couldn't make it up.'

'Well, you could. But who cares. We'll save another one for some beers after sunset later. You'll love Baianova. It's like going back in time – the Havana of the East.'

'I thought it was bombed to smithereens,' Dara said.

'Not everything. They rebuilt a lot of it and now they're looking to make it into a resort. There's even a nightclub on the roof of this ancient tower that looks out over the sea...'

'Full of the usual suspects, no doubt.'

'Stop bitching. It'll be filled with tourists soon enough if the airport is built.'

'What airport?'

'Well, from what I heard, the Zohmeans are in talks with the Chinese.'

'Are you serious?'

'Straight up. A cooperative venture that'll refurbish and update the old airstrip on the coast.'

She couldn't resist it.

'Maybe they'll run flights to Melbourne via Prague for your personal home leave convenience.'

'What do you mean, Prague?'

She stared sullenly out the window; just her and her big mouth.

'What do you mean, Dara?'

Anger filled the air-conditioned cabin of the 4Runner on both sides now like a chemical weapon.

'I found your plane ticket, *mate.*'

'Oh, yeah?'

'Yeah. Struck me as odd that your flight home to see your old Maori mum goes via United World Headquarters, duty station of the *alleged* ex.'

'You snoop through my things, it's your lookout.'

'It was on your desk. You were in your office. On the phone. You don't even care enough to hide the bloody thing.'

There was silence for the next few kilometres. His mouth was twisted into an ugly pout. She thought of a Tibetan meditative exercise she knew: consider a beautiful face, then imagine only one change to it, the same face without its layer of skin. Attraction to repulsion in the flicker of a thought. He kept his eyes on the road.

'It's the Thousand Mile Rule, darling.'

'Not one I've seen in the regulations.'

'Nah. One of the more important ones, though. Unwritten. Namely, when stationed more than one thousand miles from a spouse or partner, staff member is authorised to fool around in the field.'

'Does it authorise you to tell lies?'

'Well, if you didn't guess where I'd be going on my home leave, you were already lying to yourself.'

'Why don't you just go and fuck off.'

The cloudless sky seemed too beautiful to overhang this petty exchange.

'So, incidentally, what are your long term plans — to ride off into the sunset and live happily ever after with her? Is that it?'

Silence.

'Just wondering...' She looked at the way the sun fell across his tawny skin, creating tiny shadows from the jet black hair on his forearms. She knew him so well. And yet she didn't know him at all. And now she couldn't shut the fuck up.

'Because from what I hear, you'll regret it.'

Silence for a beat, then he muttered two words that made her even more furious.

'I know.'

'Say again?'

'I said, I *know*.'

They drove for a few kilometres along the edge of a shimmering, gorgeous sea before they came to Baianova. Of course the name had changed many times down the centuries; that was just what the Italians had called it. By the time they pulled into the Palacio Hotel grounds, they were just about speaking again. There were already four white UW vehicles in the parking lot, and on the terrace she spotted Thierry from Finance and Louise from Human Rights. Two classic thousand-milers right there.

The desk clerk confirmed that they had a 'first class' room and rattled on enough for both of them, asking them where they were from, commenting on how much he liked Nicole Kidman, and how would they believe that this very hotel had once played host to the great *Bahb Gildoff* himself in former times.

Upstairs, she swished a scorpion down the plughole, sprayed the mattress and changed the sheets, camping up the OCD routine for Conrad's amusement. He immediately lay down on the bed, unfazed by the lingering pong of insect killer.

'I hope you never have to stay in a second-class room,' he said.

She eyed a dusty contraption nestled on the window sill, before joining him. 'Do you think the air conditioner works?'

Later they sat opposite each other in a dining room that was empty and threadbare. Technicolor heyday prints and tourist posters emblazoned the walls, picturing holiday-makers sunning themselves under a flourish of Art Deco font that read: *Ben venuto a Zohmea!* They ordered fresh lobster and French fries from an unsmiling elderly man in a pressed white jacket. He placed two plates on the table noiselessly

73

with a swish of his cotton cloth. There were silver implements to eat the lobster with, in bone china dishes, each bearing the gilded name and crest of the hotel in its glory days.

Dara looked at the food. 'We're gonna burn in hell for this.'

'Why?'

'What about the starving...'

'Hey! We're supporting the local fishing co-op,' assured Conrad. 'You can have shark tomorrow.'

After a carafe of red, they considered a parting glass in the bar and an early night.

'The sun's going down...' She peered out over the balcony. 'What about a walk in the garden?'

'Tomorrow. Let's get some drinks now.'

From the lobby, however, they spotted a small group of UW staff already on the case. The women were dressed for after work cocktails in Manhattan. Four of the men were wearing Hawaiian shirts.

'The state of that bunch,' Dara said.

'It's called R&R. We work hard enough.'

'You know what?' she said. 'Let's walk into town.'

The old port boasted an extraordinary blend of architecture. They passed whitewashed Arabic archways and European neo-classical plazas. On one street they found a building like an old cinema that had a sign saying RICK'S LOUNGE. That detail alone, they decided, was worth getting drunk for.

'I hope you know the words to *La Marseillaise*,' she said.

It turned out to be a cross between a pool hall and an

old-fashioned ballroom, complete with upstairs balcony and revolving mirrored ball, which was already scattering a little magic around the walls. By degrees the place filled up with aid workers, peacekeepers, Italian pilots, doe-eyed hookers, local students, Danish explosives advisors, arms dealers, Baianova entrepreneurs and some of the older generation of Italo-Zohmeans.

The horseshoe bar itself was pure 1930s steel top, with a deco-framed mirror behind the counter arching to the ceiling, giving the effect of a giant jukebox. Its upper shelves were decorated with bottles of fancy brand name booze — all empty, as international liquor had not been imported since the Liberation. The lower ones were packed full of local beer and wine.

Its structure was like the chassis of a vintage car, with smooth, rounded corners in pearly cream Formica and two horizontal pewter lines ran the length of it a third of the way up. The original steel stools were bolted to the floor and everything was faded and glittering at the same time. The barman was a woman, attractive and a little formidable. A deep scar ran down the right side of her face from just above the level of her ear to the top of her neck and under her chin.

'I can see her as a poster girl for the revolution,' whispered Conrad.

'Oh yeah? Go on — tell her that. I dare you.'

'Nah, I like my nose. Shame about the scar though.'

'I think it makes her more beautiful.'

'Like a no-shit Xena, yeah?'

After an hour they were joined on their left by a group of jolly English speakers. There was a beautiful, ebony-plaited woman in the embrace of another with cropped blonde hair, and a rugged looking man in civvies.

'You look like the cats that got the cream,' Dara said to the women. The pair were glazed over with alcohol and looked at her with vague animosity.

'What can I say...' the man answered. 'My love life is a pint of Guinness!' This got a laugh around the bar and the women sniggered, looking more interested in each other than in their beau.

Loners, male and female, attached themselves to bar stools beside Conrad and Dara and the tables edging the dance floor filled up until people were standing at the walls. Around the room, the blast-laughter of small groups erupted every now and then.

When the power went down at ten o'clock, a generator kicked in to keep the beers cold. Towards midnight a rather ancient live jazz trio took to the small stage. After a little while Dara thought she recognised them from a faded black and white photo perched on one of the shelves of the bar. It pictured an eight-piece band in tuxedoes and dickie bows, taken maybe fifty years before. They played strange, melancholy Jazz that fused local rhythms with American swing. Then they played big band classics and some cabaret stuff, after that they went back into more music with local rhythms. Pint of Guinness Lover moved in against Conrad, whiskey glass perched on shoulder.

'I love watching white folk trying to dance African,' he grinned.

'Yeah,' Conrad agreed, as a pale couple grooved down nearby. 'It's heart warming.'

76

Conrad had hit it off big-time with the bartender after all. Her name was Rahel and she was a former combatant. After one battle, when her face was almost blown off by a piece of shrapnel, a Zohmean field surgeon had saved it in one of the legendary underground hospitals in the north. When she lined up a pair of shot glasses full of local hooch for her favourite *ferenji*, Dara had to jump up and run for the loo. She could hear laughter behind her, which was fine by her. She'd happily head back to the hotel at this point and let Rahel knock a few corners off Conrad.

On her way back, she stepped out a side door thinking to get some fresh air. Not quite. It was still around twenty-eight degrees and as usual the mosquitoes were hovering like teen boys in a disco. Humid now at sea level, the heat was still heavy and tainted with the stench of half-filled rubbish bags strewn among silver barrels. There was sand everywhere, creeping in off the street and piling up around the edges of wooden crates. As she stood there, she could still hear the music and bar chatter from inside. She looked around at the bleakness of the empty yard with its mortar-damaged walls. A distinct sense of betrayal seeped through her, followed by sadness.

She thought how cold it must be back in the open desert, in the dark. How abandoned the fighters were. The horror of it, the persistence of it, the sheer bloody legacy the mission was here to address. And it wasn't being addressed. How long would it take before they could even bury the bodies? *But we're alive...* In all of this she wondered if she had the strength to bail out on Conrad again, one more time, only this time for good.

When she came back into the ballroom, she stood for a while watching the crowd on the lowered parquet dance floor. One couple caught her eye: they almost seemed to be moving on a different plane from the melée, paying no attention to anybody else, not speaking, just dancing in each other's arms. Their movements were smooth and feline, feet matching each other's steps, a subtle twist of hip or turn of head evoking pure sensuality with an elegance that transcended their surroundings.

The woman was Zohmean, maybe in her late fifties, Modigliani features with a flame tree blossom in her hair. She wore a real summer dress and high, slim-heeled shoes that looked well-worn and well-repaired. Her hair was up in a bun, like a girl in a sepia photograph. The man was Italian, his weathered face was handsome and moustachioed. He wore a pristine white shirt, black trousers and leather shoes.

The dancers around them were not moving in formal dance steps, but in that clumsy free flow of a Saturday night prevalent pretty much anywhere in the world. People were drunk by now. Women were beautiful and glistening and men gleamed with that exciting but scary portent of sex or violence. Dara was buzzing again too, and when she looked out across the room and saw her lover, she felt that deep stab of excitement so difficult to let go of. He was standing in apparent hilarious conversation with some Gebresellassie clone at the bar. Despite herself, when he waved to her, grinning his big handsome bastard smile, she waved back. Yeah, she thought. Wave. What's a girl to do?

He must have missed her. When she reached the bar again, he grabbed her up into a snarly bear hug and covered her neck and chest with ticklish kisses. She squealed and kissed back, but only half-listened to his whiskey ramblings after that. He reminded her that as long as they were both stationed in Senara, they weren't, realistically, going to break up, now were they? So why didn't they both just take it easy and enjoy the trip? What was the point in making things complicated? He would make it up to her, he promised. They would go to Bali on his next leave, just the two of them. It would be really special.

She knocked back another one of the shots Rahel had lined up in front of them, and nodded. She was tired, they would never go to Bali, and the only thing she thought was special in the whole world was this waltzing couple, with fresh shirt and flower. They were a hint of grace in the tarnished night and, for just a moment, they had out-ghosted the savagery of the desert.

Turning round, she watched them dance a while longer, drifting on the waves of the music, lost in each other, until Conrad's arm slipped around her waist finally, pulling her away and she couldn't see them anymore.

IMAGE OF THE DAY

Tahmina waited for the computer to start up. The first task of the morning was the uploading of *Image of the Day* onto the website. Bren had been in the field the day before and said he had a perfect photo they could use.

'Here you go,' he said, handing her a printout. Tahmina took the photo into her hand. It was taken at a children's workshop in a school just south of Juba. A musical master was performing traditional music for children who may never have heard it live, as they had all been born during the conflict.

Tahmina sighed deeply. It was sad, that was all. And maddening.

She tried not to sound impatient.

'Thank you, but we can't use that,' she said.

'Why not? It's a great picture,' Bren protested.

'Don't you see what's wrong with it?'

'It's perfect. Look at the light. The kids' faces.'

'I'll give you three guesses.'

'What. You see the teacher, you see the students, the instruments…'

'Give me a minute,' she said. Tahmina walked around the office to run it by the others. Bren followed her.

'Nice,' Deepak said, glancing at it briefly.

'Beautiful,' Marisol agreed.

Carton, deep in conversation on the phone, gave a thumbs up from his desk. Tahmina looked for Noor, but she was outside having a ciggie.

'So what's wrong with the photo then?' Bren demanded.

'Weren't there any girls at the workshop?'

Bren's brow crinkled. 'Ehm, yeah.'

'So, what about our gender guidelines? Visibility for girls?'

He shrugged, looking a bit sheepish.

'Can we look at your other shots?'

Bren sighed loudly. He removed his camera from its case and turned on the viewer and they checked the images as they carouselled across the small screen. In the first one, Bren had focused from an angle to the right of the teacher, mostly because of the light, which was fair enough. But the girls were sitting in the shade under a window on the opposite wall. There was just one usable option, taken from the left shoulder of the teacher, where the viewer could clearly see several girls. It was not as technically correct.

'Let's use this one.'

'I suppose I could Photoshop it.' Bren disappeared upstairs and brought a new printout ten minutes later.

'Thanks.'

Noor was back at her desk by then. Tahmina approached her. 'What do you think of this one for *Image of the Day*?' she

81

asked, handing over the first printout. 'Everybody's approved it. Carton thinks it's great.'

Noor looked at it briefly, then glared at Tahmina.

'We can't use that!'

Tahmina smiled. 'But you and I are the only ones who have objected.'

'You don't say.'

'Bren took this one too, what do you think?' She handed Noor the second choice, enhanced now by the miracle of digital technology. In it, a row of little boys and girls listened, enchanted, to the traditional music. It was touching and it was gender balanced.

'Yes. Let's use that one.'

'I showed the first around for feedback as usual, Noor. Not one comment. Indian, Canadian, Spanish—not one of them noticed. Bren loved it.'

Noor frowned, observing the girls' faces, glowing and beautiful. She shook her head gently.

'My God,' she said. 'What hope have we got?'

OPERATION CAT LIFT

Raphael's farewell party was just kicking off when Bren and Trini reached Jacaranda Street. The Strokes were blasting over the garden wall and the smoke from a barbecue wafted out to the front of the house. The place was already full of party guests as they went inside and Raphael was just setting up the Karaoke machine.

'What's the theme tonight?' asked Luisa from the US Consulate, who had followed in behind them. 'Not another Blow-Up Halloween party?'

'It's a Goodbye Castro and Kennedy party,' Trini said.

Luisa grinned. 'Kinda late on that one, huh?'

'No, it's really sad,' Trini said. 'Raphael's getting promoted to the Nairobi office.'

'So what's sad about that?'

'Well, he can't get anyone to take in his housemates.' Trini nodded at Castro, a podgy marmalade who sat under a Flame tree on the side lawn, his half-bitten off ears twitching as he observed the humans invading his demesne, yet again. Kennedy, a slick furry shadow, sat about a metre away, her eyes narrowed in disdain. Trini sighed. 'They're so sweet.'

'Didn't one of them bite Hachiro Tanaka?'

'Well, of course they were feral,' Trini said.

Raphael threw his eyes up, and put down the Karaoke microphone.

'They're not feral now. Castro and Kennedy are perfectly house-trained pets. And they're distraught, poor little lambs.'

'Cats,' Bren said.

Raphael ignored him. 'They've been watching my trunks and boxes disappear out the front gate all day. They know I'm leaving! They are going to miss me so much.'

Everybody would miss Raphael, his prodigious music collection and his fine French wines. And they would probably miss his parties even more. They defied both the government curfew and international security guidelines — always an added attraction. Legend had it he had once thrown a Hug A Tree For Jesus party under heavy shelling in a Kabul guesthouse, and his Guy Fawkes' party, with its unusual pyrotechnics, had been a great success until the Militia arrived.

'Hey,' said Ramesh from The Innocents' Trust, 'you could always drop 'em off at Hong's Happy Wok House on the way to the airport!'

'That's not funny,' Bren told him. 'I have a theory that one in every ten humans has been a cat in another life. It's what makes them cat people.'

This was greeted with hoots of laughter, but Trini nodded in agreement.

'It's true. Raphael is a cat person.'

Raphael nodded. 'And you and Bren are cat people too, aren't you?' Raphael asked.

84

'Oh, we are,' Bren said, putting his arm around the gorgeous Trini.'That's sort of what brought us together.'

'You know, we should talk,' Raphael said. He served the happy couple two José Cuervo shots so they could get happier fast. By midnight he was laying the hard sell on them.

'I only need someone to mind them until I get settled in Nairobi,' he pleaded. 'Then I'll send for them, end of story. You've taken care of them before, while I was on leave.'

'Yes,' Trini shouted, 'but dropping by to feed them after work is different from taking them home.'

'What?'

The room was now packed with a Karaoke crowd of international aid workers, peacekeepers, their many Zohmean colleagues and the usual journo contingent, all swaying side to side in jolly unison. They had their arms round each others' shoulders, beers in hand, and were singing at the top of their lungs: 'We are the World…We are the children…'

'Are you sure you can send for them from Nairobi?' Trini bellowed.

'Of course! They are my cats, I *love* them.' Raphael said. 'Ten days tops!'

Next morning Trini was roused by an alarming crash in the sitting room. She groaned. It was way too early to be awake after a Raphael party. She rolled over, trying to remember how they'd gotten home in the end, something niggling in the back of her mind, but then there was another crash and a weird scurrying sound. Bren, of course, was asleep. She got up and walked to the door of the bedroom, opened it and screamed.

'Dios mío!'

The main room looked like it had been ransacked by a crowd of marauding baboons. Her jaw fell as she saw her beloved plaster bust of Elvis in chunks on the floor. Then she grabbed at her ankle, which was in the jaws of a marmalade cat.

'Bren-dan!'

Castro and Kennedy, thus named as they were mostly at each other's throats, quickly formed an alliance once they understood the nature of their detention in Bren and Trini's apartment. Despite their reluctant surrender to the Raphael administration, they had retained many of their street gangsta ways. Castro was bitey and Kennedy was scratchy. True Zohmeans, their determination to cause havoc in the enemy camp could only be described as revolutionary. They peed in the middle of the floor. They ripped the frilly sofa covers to shreds and knocked over lamps. They stole and ate a cooked chicken, then threw it up all over Trini's Persian rug. And that was just the beginning.

Raphael wrote apologetic, useless emails from Nairobi.

'Can you get your hands on a can of mushy peas?' he wrote.'They love them.' Or, 'a large cardboard box will while away Castro's afternoon nicely'.

Getting the cats to Nairobi was proving nearly impossible. Bren went to see Halima in Travel, which made him happy. He had always secretly fancied beautiful Halima, although he found her a bit scary.

'They need exit papers,' she said, deadpan.

'You're kidding, right?'

'To get the exit papers, you need a certificate of good health,' she snorted. 'Signed by a qualified vet. And the last veterinarian in Zohmea defected six months ago to Dubai with a singer from a Filipino boy band.'

The last two words came out in italics.

'Thanks, Halima.'

'Good luck with that.' Her eyes followed him down the room as he walked out. But not in a good way.

It wasn't long before Bren and Trini became the favourite *ferenji* joke of the clerks in the Customs Office downtown. Whenever either of them arrived, the boys' faces would light up, forms and rubber stamps at the ready. One Thursday afternoon, Trini walked in briskly, having procured the signature of a visiting animal health expert. She figured she had it in the bag.

'It has to be signed,' the clerk told her.

'But it's already signed,' Trini countered.

'Hmm,' the clerk replied. 'But it is signed here, in *this* box and it needs to be signed there in *that* box.'

It was more than a month before the email they had been waiting for arrived. It was as short as it was mysterious:

> *US Marines to the rescue, HOO-ray! Incoming tomorrow a.m. Dip jet 08:00—put C & K on same for ret. flight 19:00 hrs. Military airport parking—Lieut. Gary will do honours. Texan. Brick. Shithouse. Can't miss him.*

The only incoming flight the following day was a diplomatic jet bearing a top-level UW official, who was in Senara to chair a meeting between the Zohmean People's Front and the People's Front of Zohmea. It would return to Odalia via the logistic base at Lokichoggio, departing from the Zohmean International airport at nineteen hundred. From Loki, a Yemeni volunteer would get the cats to the Kenyan capital by truck. Bren and Trini's mission, should they choose to accept it, was to infiltrate the airport with the cats and hand them over to the US operative for a covert passage to freedom.

'Easy, right?' Bren said to Hachiro, as they sat in the cafeteria.

'You are both insane.'

'Raphael has organised everything on the other end…'

'Raphael couldn't organise his way out of a paper bag,' Hachiro pointed out.

'Well, he's close to Sorensen's assistant.'

'Have you ever meet Sorensen?'

'No.'

'We are talking international incident.'

'Hey,' Bren said, considering the Persian rug, Trini's infected leg and the stench in the apartment. 'What's the worst that can happen?'

By 3pm, 'Operation Cat Lift' had advanced on several fronts. There were sleeping tablets from Stalker, the ex-Special Forces guy. There was a strategy from Amado, the Ghanian Air Ops clerk.

'You won't get in through our Security,' he told them. 'So you'll need to try the old Zohmean military entrance.'

'Really?' Bren asked. For the first time, he felt a little flutter in his stomach.

'Sure. There's a gate around the side, way down the old road. Drive as far as you can go, turn right, down again — and there's a hut and a barrier.'

'And an armed Zohmean Revolutionary Guard?' Trini asked.

'Yeah, that too,' Amado said. 'But you're on your own there.'

'Okay, let's do it,' Trini said, finally. It wasn't just a rescue mission any longer. Those fucking cats had to go.

The afternoon had cooled nicely as the vehicle arrived at the old military area of the airport. A lone Zohmean guard with an AK47 was hunkering down, listening to a transistor radio. He had that understated, wiry look of pure power that distinguished the Zohmean military. They stopped the vehicle ten feet before the barrier.

'Salam!' Trini beamed, alighting from the 4Runner. 'We're just hoping to get into the car park here for a few minutes…'

The soldier lowered his chin and looked up at her from an odd angle, which rendered him vaguely psychotic.

'Purpose of visit?'

'We need to get something to one of Ambassador Sorensen's assistants,' Bren said. He was going for authoritative, but it came out scared shitless.

The guard scowled. Then he looked at Trini with that part salacious, part fascinated stare that men in khaki affect when confronted with an unarmed female.

'What is in car?'

'Ehm…' Trini stammered.

'What is in car?' He marched around the back of the vehicle.

'Open.' He motioned towards it with a casual sweep of his weapon, kicking the bumper.

As soon as the back door opened and the air-conditioned comfort was sucked out of the vehicle, something rather terrifying happened. A feeble, but plaintive feline cry sounded from the container in the back.

'Mierda,' Trini thought.

The soldier stepped forward, tipped the box with his gun, cocked his head, flexed his eyebrows and stepped back. Then he broke into a grin.

'Mieuw,' he said.

'Mieuw?' Trini repeated, puzzled. 'Ai, madre, sí, *Mieuw!*'

'Cats,' Bren said.

'Take out.' The soldier's voice sounded tough, but he was still grinning.

Bren lifted the crate out of the back of the car, turned it around, and the soldier peered inside, to be confronted by two whiskered creatures becoming more forceful in their protests. The soldier waggled his fingers playfully in front of the mesh panel, clicking his tongue.

'Name?'

'Ahm. Castro and —' Bren stalled for a moment; never say you're American. 'Bobby Sands.'

The soldier stepped back, let out that unfettered howl of mirth that only Zohmeans can, and slapped his AK with gusto. Trini stepped back a tad.

'Revolution!' he roared.

'Oh, yes, indeed,' Bren said. 'You have no idea.'

'Visas?' the soldier giggled, nodding his head in the direction of the cats.

'Visas?' Trini sputtered. 'They don't even have *passports!*'

The soldier responded with another cackle and slapped Bren on the back manfully, giving him the official Zohmean rebel handshake.

'Revolution Cat!'

'Catstro!' Trini shrieked, impressed at her own pun.

'Bobby Sand! Britash Imperiahl-ism!' The guard slapped one fist hard into an open palm and laughed again, the barrel of his weapon swinging around with gay abandon.

Trini curled an interrogatory nostril at Bren. He shrugged. How could he explain the Bobby Sands reference? Inspires Afro-Hibernian solidarity every time.

Suddenly the soldier stopped grinning. Trini had a ghastly thought. She made a face at Bren, rubbing imaginary money between the tips of her fingers behind the soldier's back. Bren shook his head hysterically. 'Shut up!' he mouthed.

The guard nodded at the car and then looked directly at Bren, brows even.

'You bring me?' he said, in a low voice. Bren gaped, trying to figure out whether or not it was a trick question. The soldier stared Bren down. Now Bren *was* scared shitless.

Then the guard smiled again, slowly. 'Okay,' he said.

'Okay?'

'Okay.' Then he stood a moment, angling his head in reflective pose. 'The Prophet, peace be upon him. He love cats,' he told them.

'I've heard that,' Trini said, moved.

'Access fifteen minute.' He was getting tough again. 'Fifteen only.'

'Thank you,' Bren said. 'You know, I have this theory…'

'Bren!' Trini screeched, pulling at his Bermuda shorts to get him back to the vehicle.

The soldier stood back and walked coolly over to the barrier rope, lifting it with some ceremony — no longer amused. He was a Zohmean Revolutionary Guard; his decision was sovereign. Not to mention fortunate. Bren saluted him as they drove through slowly. Trini flashed him the Costaverden national smile.

'What was that 'shut up' stuff about?' she asked.

'You could have got us shot for trying to corrupt an official,' he told her.

'What?'

'This is The People's Democratic Republic of Zohmea. Possibly the only honourable revolution. No way is that man going to stoop to taking bribes from foreign imperialist fools.'

'You're right,' Trini sighed. 'I love this country.'

They drove over to the row of military and UW vehicles at the edge of the old fenced-in air strip. Trini chopped up a whole sleeping tablet this time and mashed it into two balls of food, feeding it to them through the mesh.

'Escucha, guys,' she told them. 'You gotta behave yourselves from now on if you ever want to see your querido Raphael again!'

Right on cue, they spotted the convoy approaching up the airport road in the distance. The last car peeled off sneakily from the rest and headed their way. It pulled up near them carefully, nose to the fence.

There was almost complete silence, except for the insects buzzing in the brush. Trini looked at Bren and they slowly opened the doors of their car and walked into the open compound. The concrete expanse, with clumps of grass erupting from cracks in the old slabs, was still warm from the heat of the day. Around the edges of some closed-down hangars, there were jeep husks, a burned-out rocket launcher, and some more dead war hardware.

After a minute, a massive, desert-fatigued military officer in his late forties emerged from the other UW vehicle. He stood up fully, which was pretty full, and began to walk towards them. Three words spontaneously entered the mind of each civilian. Texan. Brick. Shithouse.

'Hoo-RAY...' Trini thought.

With a towering gait and a face that only a mother could love, the Marine looked left, right and behind him. Then he leaned in towards Bren and Trini, who leaned in too. It was a rugger huddle of conspiracy.

'So,' he drawled. 'Have you got ... the *kitties*?'

Mirth galloped up Bren's throat and he drew his hand up over his mouth giving a cough instead. He straightened up.

'Yes, sir!'

Trini, whose shoulders were shaking visibly, turned and opened up the trunk of their car. The Marine opened the back of his vehicle.

Bren slotted the cat crate silently into the space within, and the Marine closed the trunk again. Trini noticed that there was silence from the crate during this procedure. Trini one, The Verve nil.

Lt Gary turned and sat back into his air conditioned car. It started up, they caught a brief salute through the window, then he disappeared across the concrete towards the airport's new terminal. Bren and Trini watched him depart, like Ethan Edwards in khakis, lit by a slanting sun.

'So?' Hachiro hissed as they filed into the staff meeting the next morning.

'No news yet,' Bren admitted. 'Bit worried.'

'No shit,' Hachiro said. 'What are you going to do?'

'Get drunk tonight,' Bren answered.

'Well, that's a start.'

It was a long day, checking and re-checking emails. Nada. No texts. All day long, Bren wondered if they would be fired. Whether Lt Gary could be court-martialled. Whether Bobby Sands had eaten Castro during the flight. Whether Raphael would be re-posted to North Korea. Trini had received nothing on her end either. They'd arranged to meet after work, and he was relieved, finally, to close his computer.

On his way down the main corridor, Bren passed Halima. She gave him a funny look.

'So, Bren, the cats flew away to Kenya?'

He turned around, smiling. 'Yeah, mental, huh?'

She half-smiled, made as if to move off, then swung back. 'By the way…'

'Yeah?' he was still grinning. He'd always wondered how long her hair was under that veil.

'Will you get me a passport?'

'A passport?' he echoed. It was a bit like what the Zohmean guard had said.

'I only have my little blue UW Laissez-Passez, you see. And it says I am Stateless.'

His face dropped.

'I was born in a refugee camp and I'll probably never travel on a diplomatic jet.'

'Jesus, Halima, I'm … I'm sorry.'

She started to walk back up the corridor. 'But it's a good story, right, Bren?'

Bren crinkled up his eyes. Shit. He stood for a minute, ass well and truly kicked.

'Hey, Bren!' It was Halima again, starting up the far staircase, neat in shadow form against a window. 'It's okay.'

'No, wait, Halima …' he shouted, but she had already disappeared half-way up the stairs. He sat down for a moment. They'd facilitated the safe transit of two skinny domestic cats to a leafy suburb in Nairobi. How funny was that, really.

It was Friday night at 'The Restful Prodder,' and the crowd up at the bar were already in a state of advanced merriment by the time Trini and Bren arrived to drown their fears about Operation Cat Lift.

The old shoe factory building that housed the deminers' club was packed with the most diverse gathering of souls in the capital. You could find a Consul General in conversation with a member of the French Foreign Legion, or a Ukranian pilot chatting up a political affairs officer. Trini spotted their crowd already in heated conversation near a window. As Bren and Trini approached, however, the drinkers turned serious. Jedidiah Henley, Head of AirOps, stood up and put his beer on the table, looking like he'd been waiting for them.

'So,' he said in his Jamaican treacle voice. 'You put two felines in the luggage compartment of the Ambassador's jet.'

They said nothing.

'You should know,' he continued, 'that half way to Lokichoggio, those babies began to howl, goodo ...'

Trini's heart was pulsating rapidly. She might need her heart medicine. Or a tequila shot.

'Do you know how many people in the organisation this potentially affects?'

Bren sweated. Hachiro's words, *international incident*, were zinging around in his head.

'I don't know what you think you were up to, but an hour ago, I received a communication direct from Loki ...'

Faces looked on with deep concern.

'Ambassador Sorensen actually *heard* those bloody animals caterwauling.'

'He did?' Bren said. He needed tequila.

'Yes, everybody heard them, apparently. Yowling and howling. In a UW diplomatic jet.' Jed's face was stony.

'So what did Sorensen do?' Trini asked, eyes wide.

'The Senior Representative to Odalia demanded to know what was going on. He was briefed by Lt Col Gary Bradstone, officer on Secondment from the US Marines. And when he heard about this disgraceful act of insubordination ...'

Somebody giggled at the bar. Jed gave them a dirty look.

'When he heard what was making the noise,' he continued, but then broke down himself, shaking his head and crinkling up his eyebrows into a laugh, 'the stupid man *smiled*."

'Smiled?' Trini repeated. People had now started to laugh behind Jed.

'Smiled – and then he stuck his nose back into his damn report,' Jed concluded, shaking his head. 'You smart asses are damn lucky. '

'Wow,' Bren said. 'We did it.'

Jed leaned in closer towards the pair of them, lowering his voice. 'Sure – and I don't know how, but you two - and that crazy bastard Raphael – should all be busted.' He stepped back.

'YES,' he mocked, beginning to laugh again, apparently with gusto. 'You did. And you'd better celebrate *tonight* in case the Chief of Mission hears about it in the morning ... '

So it was going to be a fun evening at 'The Restful Prodder' after all. Bren ordered two tequilas and grinned at Trini. He knew she knew what he was going to say.

'One in ten,' Trini agreed.

MARE RUBRUM

Maura was slowly awoken by an absence of sound. It was the same early hour that she usually woke, but she was not in her own bed this morning. She blinked at a large ceiling fan whirling above, and remembered she was on the coast. The roar of the MiG jets was missing. Every dawn for weeks now in the capital, she had been awakened by that distinctive scream of burning fuel made on take-off by the nation's fighter planes. They sounded like giant blowtorches scorching out over the air base, the soundtrack to what the BBC had described as 'the impending renewal of hostilities'.

She threw the sheet away from her and lay on her back. There was a sound, though, muted and repetitious. It inspired rest; it complemented this state of half-sleep. She relaxed again, and returned to it with slow recognition — the sea. The creep of water up a beach, the neat slap of the tide against the sand, and the swirling, mellifluous drag backwards to meet the next surge.

The relief of a day without the bombs and dust of the city made her not want to waste it. She walked into the bathroom, checked for scorpions in the shower and let the water rinse away the heat of the night. Then she pulled on a pale linen dress and her hat and grabbed a towel.

At the back of her mind, the reason for her visit lingered like a bad dream. But since it was a Sunday, she at least had twenty-four hours before she had to address the task ahead. To keep a low profile, she had chosen one of the older local hotels. The brand new concrete and glass one in town was for the sociable set; the so-called 'resort' out on the beach was off the main drag and pretty run-down. It catered to volunteers, illicit lovers and gun-runners.

She herself had come as hatchet-bearer. Following orders from the People's Democratic Republic of Zohmea that all international aid organisations leave the country within ten days, she had been sent to close the organisation's coastal field office. The Zohmean staff who had worked so hard for five years with some of the country's most vulnerable war victims would not only lose their jobs, but risk detention as collaborators after the exodus.

The door dragged along the stone floor as she tried to open it, pulling in sand that had scattered across the veranda in the night. Its wood was old and warped, almost no paint left to speak of, since the hotel had lain vacant during the decades of war. A jumble of roses had grown wild over the filigree woodwork of the balcony and in an open sky the sun was ascending from the horizon of a calm, blue expanse.

Maura looked around and closed her eyes, imagining what it must have been like when it was a resort. The garden surrounding the massive Italian villa would have been splendid. At one end of the shallow bay there was a pier that must have been bobbing with boats, and at the other, where her room was, the cabins facing the shore would have been modern and bright. Now there was a forsaken enchantment to the early morning beach. *Mare Rubrum* — the Red Sea.

She walked down and sat a few feet from the waves, imagining the galleys that had once brought spices and silks from Adulis to Asia Minor, and on to Persia and China. How many wars since then? How many lives and dreams lost below the same horizon? It had been a while now since her mind had wandered like this, and she happily let it stray.

Watching the strengthening light shimmer like liquid across the surface of the water, she gradually felt the heat build on her shoulders and head. She let her hands rest on her knees until the quiet began to break up with the sounds of port machinery down the shore; shards of conversation from the dining room in the villa.

The port was partially operational, but like the whole country, its potential had never been fulfilled due to the conflict. Cargo cranes stood motionless along the quays; the roads in and out of the town had almost no traffic. It struck her that living here sometimes felt like heaving through the last days of a cancerous patriarch, who was strangling his own children in death's throes. A salt and seaweed tang filled her senses and then the familiar cry of a seagull brought her back into the present.

Out of the corner of her eye, she became aware of a man walking slowly in her direction along the water's edge. Interesting, she thought. Blond-headed, another *ferenji*. Part of her was irked at having to share the beach, and another part was intrigued at who would be up this early on a Sunday morning.

The man stopped and smiled, crooking his head, as if requesting her approval to approach. She smiled back, not moving. He walked slowly toward her, bent down at her side and stretched out a hand. In his palm, a tiny green and black starfish quivered, droplets of salt water in its intricate patterns.

'Oh!' she said. She was completely captivated. He gestured and she let him take her hand.

'For you,' he said, resting it into her palm.

She looked at the starfish, then at the man, who was watching her and smiling.

'Beautiful?' he asked.

'Yes, beautiful!' She examined its convoluted design. Shades of gold, black and lime all glinted from its tiny form. She had never seen one before and it was quite perfect. The man's eyebrows crinkled into a quizzical arch, as if now seeking her consent to stay.

'Thank you.' She smiled, and then again more broadly when he sat down. His hair, close up, was more silver than blond, and his eyes shone with a blend of scepticism and surprise, as if he were as astonished to find her as she was to see him.

She brushed the starfish with her finger, and when it moved she felt an army of tiny sucker pads move on her palm, squealed and started to laugh. His own infectious laugh billowed around her and she found herself curiously at ease.

He said nothing for a while, and it was clear that he spoke almost no English. But he was willing to make the most of what he knew.

'Beautiful!' he said, indicating the sea in front of them.

'Waves,' she said.

'I love. Always.'

'The oldest sound.'

'Yes,' he said. 'But also new. Every time new. And new and new and new.'

He said it with drawn-out, somewhat grandiose emphasis, echoing the movement of the surf with small gestures of his hand and head.

'You are from Russia?'

'Hmm…something like that,' he said, grinning as if challenging her to guess. Maura tried to remember which post-Soviet independent ran the planes for UW.

'Georgia?'

He clicked his tongue and threw his eyes up to heaven, in mock horror.

'Ukraine!' she corrected.

He nodded his head. 'You are English?'

'Nothing like that!' she frowned, mimicking him.

'Ha! Irish!' He was chuffed that he'd guessed correctly, and they shook hands in a conspiratorial bargain. So, he was one of the pilots on the United World carrier flights. The crews based in Khartoum rented cabins in the hotel on a long-term basis and their mates from routes around Africa joined them from time to time on R&R. They piloted old Russian Antonovs mostly, transporting anything from supplies, aid workers, military, refugees and often, according to rumour, armaments.

He didn't seem like a typical military man, but that didn't mean much. She had given up trying to define people out here. In the field you never knew. Right now he was just a guy in a bathing suit, with a great face and a skewed sense of joy that she did not care to fault.

They left the starfish on her towel and walked along the beach. Communication eased into a flirty blend of gesture and speech. He had a habit of repeating certain words to emphasise them, and he didn't seem to tire of trying to make her laugh.

'I drive plane.' He indicated this with full visual embellishment.

'Where?'

'Khartoum – Juba. Juba – Khartoum. Lokichoggio – Darfur ... '

'Oh, the nice places?' she asked.

'Very nice.'

'How about a flight for me?'

'Hmm… Sure. Where you want, Madame?'

'How about Hawaii?'

'No problem, I take.'

'No, wait—Zanzibar!'

'Sure. For you, first class. Vodka: free, free—no question asked.'

'No question asked.' She was delighted. 'Frequent flyer miles too?'

He grinned back, not comprehending.

After a late breakfast of sugary black tea and flat Arabic bread with honey, they set out to walk along a ghost promenade nearby. At one end, they broke into a decrepit bungalow that overlooked a private jetty, once the holiday home of the former dictator. There was still even a cluster of tubular steel bar stools visible in their watery grave beneath the balcony, the end to a party that the revolution had quashed, and never forgotten.

At the end of the pier, he took her hand and without words they walked in a pleasing silence. When it got too hot, they went for a swim, the calm allowing them to venture quite far from the shore. The biblical sails of some wooden dhows, ancient as the sea itself, bobbed back and forth in the distance, and every now and then she caught sight of military trucks making their way up the long coast road from the airport.

But besides that they were alone; even the choppers were taking a day off.

'Of course, no swim Mogadishu,' he told her.

'No?'

'No. Plenty shark.'

'What?'

He began to laugh.

'You think there are sharks here?'

'No — they on holiday Somalia.'

'Jesus…' she swam as fast as she could back to the shore.

They went to her room to shower, and stood in a besotted embrace beneath the water before moving to the bed. He caressed her face with his hand, crinkling his eyes, pronouncing, 'beautiful!' They spent the rest of the afternoon under the whirr of the ceiling fan, closing the shutters to deflect the intensity of the daytime heat.

She surfaced somewhere around five in the afternoon, and watched him in the fading light as he slept. He wasn't young, and in fact quite a bit older than she had originally thought. He bore deep lines on a face that was still striking and had probably been handsome, but had lost its way somewhere down the line. It was the face of a junkie, or an actor.

When he knocked on the door later to pick her up for dinner, he was wearing plain khaki pants and an old-fashioned waistcoat, adding a somewhat surreal touch of Graham Greene to the evening. And why not, Maura thought, shielding her head against the mosquitoes with a cream-coloured cotton hat.

They walked through a maze of narrow, winding streets with whitewashed walls. In the absence of street lighting, sporadic haloes of oil lanterns illuminated the craggy faces of men in conversation on the steps of carved wooden doorways. Smells of spicy frying came from a myriad of courtyards and above them, minarets and crosses alternated against the sky.

In a small plaza at the meeting of three streets near the harbour, they found seats at one of four tables lit by a string of low-watt bulbs slung overhead. They ate fresh white fish that had been brought in that day on the boats, served off an open fire. Lemon juice and bottled water accompanied the meal, since the fishermen did not serve alcohol. Every now and then he poured an inch of potent vodka into their tumblers, adding an illicit edge to the proceedings.

A three-quarter moon had risen by the time they made their way back to the resort to play at being lovers: no better game. They opened the shutters in her room and climbed in under the net. Questions simmered somewhere in her mind: family, future, past. She bet he knew the current wholesale rate for a functional RPG-29, but why would she ask.

'Tomorrow, I go Khartoum,' he said later.

'Okay. I have never been to Khartoum.'

'I not stay there. Go Chad.'

105

'Chad?'

'A new route. Not so good,' he grimaced, shaking his head.

'No kidding!'

'What mean?' he asked, frowning. Maura made a few attempts to explain herself, and settled on 'I understand.'

'Ah,' his eyes crinkled.

'I'm leaving too. I've been PNG'd,' she told him.

'P-N-G?'

'When the Government decides you are a bad person — and you must leave the country. They say you are *persona non grata*.'

'You very bad person!' he challenged, laughing.

'No seriously — they throw you out. After five years, I have to leave.'

'I am sorry. Where go?'

She sighed and shrugged her shoulders. 'Oh, you know — Khartoum, Juba. Lockichoggio maybe.'

'The nice places?'

She pushed him back on the pillow and tickled him in the ribs.

Her sleep was fitful, and despite the ceiling fan, she was too warm. Waking with a start before dawn, she was filled with nervous anticipation, waiting for the roar of the warplanes. But only a foghorn sounded out in the bay. For a moment it took her right home; she longed for the cold, pure mist of her own sea. She turned around onto her back. He had felt her restlessness, and stroked her face.

'Every morning, in the capital, at this time,' she explained.

'I hear the sound of MiG jets taking off. They always wake me.'

'MiGs? I drive!'

She waited a moment, not sure she understood what he meant.

'You fly MiG jets?'

'Before.'

'Before where?' It came out too sharply.

He hesitated. 'Afghanistan…'

Maura sat up in the bed, frowning, and drew her knees up under her chin.

'Before, long time…'

'Ah.' She couldn't think of any way to respond, and just stared through the mosquito net into the darkness.

'Long time…'

He turned his back to her and rolled on his side, facing out towards the sea in silence. When she lay back down, he didn't turn to embrace her. She didn't touch him.

She considered this stranger. Earlier, she had watched his face in sleep. Admittedly, there was something about it that she had half-hoped would never be explained to her. And yet.

Here is a man who brought me a starfish on a beach at dawn.

No more and no less. Enough, maybe. She thought of how they'd found the starfish on the way back from dinner, where she had abandoned it on the towel at the water's edge. They'd returned it to the sea, but it was dying; its vibrant colours bleaching down to faded ochre.

She pulled up close to him then, reached her arm around his chest to hug him. He took her hand in his and held onto it, and they stayed like that until they slept again.

Around dawn, he lifted the white net carefully and slipped outside it, pulling on his clothes and shoes. She feigned sleep. Before he left, through the mosquito net, he kissed the back of her hand, and she felt the star of his breath on her skin as the door of the room closed behind him.

She listened to the waves through the open window, to this sound they both loved, apparently; the oldest sound, but also new, and new, and new…

REPRISAL

Emerging from the darkened office, Emily stopped at the edge of the lawn and gazed into an adamantine Afghan sky. She let her bag slide to the ground and released her shoulders, succumbing to the deep stillness of a billion stars. Pulling in the crisp air, her exhalation produced a brief curl of breath. Autumn. The Hindu Kush stood immutable between the earth and the sky, too mighty for argument, too tough for fear; somehow comforting. It was almost seven o'clock, barely time to get home before curfew.

Picking up her bag, she moved quickly towards the exit. The trees that had made the United World compound pleasant during the warmer season were undressing slowly. Sap receded deep inside their very branches as if the party was over now and winter would brook no greenery.

Soon there would be snow and smelly paraffin heaters. Her heels echoed on the concrete of the walkway as she made her way to the entrance yard. Azad was waiting for her in the big white land cruiser and lifted his hand off the steering wheel in greeting, starting the engine as she got in the back. They stopped before the gate, waited as the security guards opened and looked into the boot, then under the engine hood. She smiled at the familiar face of the young Tajik as he passed a broad rectangular mirror attached to a broom handle underneath the car's chassis.

'Tashkoor,' said Emily.

'Khahesh mekonam!' he responded, glancing only briefly at her, but smiling.

Like everyone else, she was used to the security routines, but lately the increase in attacks had begun to permeate the 'it's okay, I'm not military' veneer worn by the civilian staff. Earlier that week a pregnant diplomat had been abducted from a security-cleared café. The week before, NGO joggers had been held up at gunpoint by a twelve-year-old. Well, she thought. That nicely nixed her idea of taking up an early morning run.

'Have you driven one of the armoured vehicles yet, Azad?'

'No, not yet,' he said. 'The drivers call them 'Elvis' cars!'

'Elvis?'

'Rock 'n' roll!'

'Oh, right,' she laughed at the accuracy. She thought of the weighty lurch and sway of a fully-armoured vehicle. 'Sometimes I think I'd feel a bit safer, though!'

'That is true, but they are so difficult to drive.'

She leaned back and tried not to think of the IED they'd reported at the morning briefing; two British squaddies dead. Young. A mobile phone detonation in an outpost that had previously known nothing remotely as sophisticated.

It was the first time in three months she'd seen any kind of tangible reaction from the four military brass at the other side of the conference table. Technology was advancing into the provinces with alarming speed. Despite the fact that up to now there had been no incidents involving the urban office vehicles, there was no denying what a deeply disturbing experience it was, as a civilian, to drive through a militarised city. Potholes and rubble by day, flood-lit desolation by night. Armed guards at most gateways, and the only new homes, ghastly in their pink and gold vulgarity, belonged to drug lords and arms dealers. Not exactly the scenic route.

The car crawled past the International Peace and Security Contingent Base 1, which was barricaded behind a high concrete wall topped with razor coils and punctuated with manned watchtowers.

Giant lighted panels along the road bathed the night in an unnatural brightness. It was pure science fiction. She felt like she was in one of those blockbusters where the world is coming to an end, all taking place in some military hinterland. Except that it wasn't the end of the world, it was just another drive home on a Wednesday night.

She glanced down at the printout of the latest Security Directive on her lap. 'Internationals permitted to reside in security-cleared guesthouses only. No unauthorised movement outside the Designated Security Parameter (DSP). No movement permitted after curfew, 19:00 hrs. No use of external transport of any kind. No walking in the city centre. Market shopping strictly prohibited.' The usual stuff.

They were making their way through a sort of conflict-hewn canyon now, where both sides of the street were piled high with IPASC Hesco bags. Azad was driving at a snail's pace, nerve-wracking at the best of times.

'It's a late meeting at the Presidential Palace,' Azad explained. 'The traffic is bad until after Base 2.'

'Well, they have plenty to talk about.' There was a regulation somewhere about expressing personal views, but fuck it. Azad looked at her in the rear-view mirror a couple of times and then spoke.

'What did you think of the apology today, Emily Jan?'

She sighed. It was a fair question. All afternoon the country had waited for the International Forces' Commander in Chief to issue an apology for the massacre of a wedding party gathered in a mountain village two days previously. When it came, he pronounced it from his own air-conditioned office over a live stream to a press conference in D.C. Never mind the bereaved and their dead babies, she thought. Semi-apologise — why don't you — to a bunch of journos on another continent.

'I think he should have apologised to the family.'

'Yes.'

Shame was not part of her job description, but she felt it anyway. And she wasn't the only one. 'We all think that, Azad.'

'Of course, Emily Jan, thank you for saying.'

The unease in the office had been muted but palpable. The Internationals were angry, the Afghan staff coolly polite. Twice that afternoon they'd played 'spot the blast' — you heard the distant boom, and you tried to guess where the device had gone off.

'South Marketplace,' Stefano had guessed first time, and he was right. The second one was closer to home and more troubling. Then there were the really creepy ones you didn't even hear, but occasionally felt, like nudges from the tendril of some demon beyond your line of vision.

'How are the studies going, Azad? Political Science, right?'

'Yes. But they will be a bit more difficult for a time now. I am a father again!'

'That's great! When?'

'My wife had baby boy, two days ago. He is wonderful.'

She stared through the glass at the armoured men and women posted at intervals along the street outside. American soldiers, their ruddy cheeks illuminated in the phosphorous-white light. They looked bored, but it was an edgy, volatile boredom, their faces as stiff as their Kevlar vests.

A kid at the checkpoint near the Italian Embassy indicated for Azad to roll down the window, with his weapon. She lowered her own window immediately.

'We're both UW staff, Corporal.' She tried to calm the pique in her voice. The American ignored her.

'I need ID, Sir. Show me your ID.'

For once, Azad's ID wasn't around his neck, and Emily winced as he reached into the glove compartment. The soldier moved back a foot, eyes glued to Azad, finger glued to his trigger. As Azad held out his badge, the kid took his time examining it, and barely glanced at Emily's.

Then he jerked his gloved hand at the road and they moved on. Azad turned on the radio, which squawked security and transport messages for the rest of the trip. After ten minutes, they pulled up outside the guesthouse.

'Congratulations on the new baby, Azad. Please give your wife my best.'

'Thank you!' Azad put his hand on his heart and smiled.

She waited in the car until one of the perimeter guards

had unbolted the door in the iron gate, emerged, checked the laneway all around, and motioned with an old Kalashnikov for her to go inside. It was every bit as menacing as the American kid's state of the art weapon. Then the guard came in behind her and slammed the bolt across again, moving back into the shadows at the side of the entrance in silence.

As she passed the gatehouse, little Karim, the youngest of the staff, stuck his head out the window.

'Goood eefning!' he called, flashing a broad Hazara smile. Up to now the only English she had ever heard from him was the joyous pronouncement, 'Heh-low. I am Karim, Handy Man!'

She shouted back. 'Goood eeevening, Karim!' The strain of the trip home began to leave her.

The guesthouse was known as 'Rose Haven,' much to the amusement of other ex-pats, and the scepticism of friends and relatives at home.

But it was a haven of sorts. The main building was a once-fashionable villa, with a long row of former stables opposite that had been converted into single accommodation units. Emily sometimes tried to imagine the garden when it was beautiful: a sixties Bond Babe villa. Now the grass was patchy and the footpaths crumbling, it was more like Miss Havisham's last stand. With typical *ferenji* audacity, there was a wooden pergola down one end, covered in Persian rugs and cushions. Late night Thursdays it was a cocoon for snuggling bodies, PX liquor and field stories. Party nights, it became a Go-Go dancers' cage.

Once past the guardhouse, Emily pulled off the long silk scarf that covered her head and plucked the pins out of her copper hair, letting it fall loose and unruly on her shoulders. She shook her head back and felt the pressure of a light headache lift, savouring the tiny symbolic moment. As she walked down the path, she breathed in the scent of the dozens of overgrown rose bushes that were wafting the last of their evening scent. The rose beds were partially lit by a saffron glow coming from Raphael's room.

He was leaning in his doorway perfectly relaxed, holding an elegant glass of red wine that was obviously not his first of the evening. Ella Fitzgerald singing 'Night and Day' floated soulfully across the Kabouli air, and a lean grey cat curled between his ankles and slinked away into the dark.

'Bonsoir, Mademoiselle!'

She smiled. Raphael, the academic who was really a music hound.

'Ça va bien, Prof?'

'The situation is delicate,' he whispered.

'Which one?'

'The roses. They are fragile now, the petals sensitive to each little gust of wind.'

'I hate autumn,' she reached out to one of the flowers, and two petals fell away from the stem.

'They have listened one too many times to Rumi.'

'And what did Rumi have to say?'

'He said, "live where you fear to live".'

'You're sentimental this evening, Raphael.'

He rolled the wine round in the glass, and looked out at the shadowy garden. 'Do you know that roses originated here?' he said. He was speaking in an uncharacteristically low tone that she could hardly hear. 'From ancient Ariana and

Persia. The Garden of Islam brought us our most beautiful flower. Imagine ...'

The howl of a helicopter overhead flying into the base nearby drowned out the rest of Raphael's words. He looked at his feet, barely concealing the disquiet evoked by the low-flying chopper. Francis Ford Coppola had a lot to answer for, thought Emily, but he'd got it right. She walked over to Raphael in his solitary doorway.

'There's some people hanging out in the dining room — Inga just texted. Will you join us for a drink?'

Raphael smiled again, his splendid bon vivant aura restored. She planted a kiss on his rosy cheek before walking on.

Nearer the main building, Monsieur Yasin was pushing his creaky bicycle towards her along the path, on his way home. He gave her a nod. He was a kindly and courteous man who kept them all fed. Tahir, the house manager, had told Emily once how he'd been a celebrated chef in Paris for years until 1992, when his wife and two of his kids were killed in a West Kabul battle. Then he'd come home to care for a daughter that had survived, blind and disabled.

'What have you cooked for us this evening, Monsieur Yasin?'

'You guess, and tell me in the morning! The vegetarians will not like it!' He gave a chortle. 'À demain, alors!'

As she entered the main house, the lights in the hallway dimmed down almost to nothing, then with splendid City Power trickery, they fizzed up again moments later. Fuck it, she'd left her iPod charging. She should really go and un-plug it. But she needed food and another hour wouldn't make much of a difference.

In the dining room, a somewhat heated exchange was ensuing.

'Come on, Philippe. The ceremony tomorrow will declare eight whole kilometres of former city wasteland landmine free. There's a school in the middle of it, and an orphanage. And it's residential. All you can eat photo ops.'

'Look, it's just not what the agency goes for,' Philippe said, huddled over his can of beer like a teenager. Emily moved his bag of equipment from a dining room chair to the window seat and sat down, smiling at the Leica still hanging from his neck.

'Why not?' protested Freshta, an area manager with The Innocents' Trust. Emily scooped a cup of pilau from one pot, followed by a cup of Monsieur Yasin's surprise casserole from another, and joined the table.

Freshta was flushed and spat her words at Philippe. 'Why must you always look for the negative? For once, this is a positive story. Just admit it. Just report a damned real story that isn't about destruction — or that isn't sanitised press office bullshit.'

'Well, that's exactly it. It's not a story. It's a PR exercise.' Philippe drank from his can, sullen.

'I know these EOD guys,' Mohammed said. 'They've trained for years, and they've worked for fifteen months on this project. They are totally dedicated. So what does their accomplishment effectively mean? Means that kids taking a shortcut to school over a wall won't get their legs blown off.'

'And in the next sector over, where the mines aren't cleared, some kid still gets it in the morning...'

'Oh, well—we might as well all go fucking home then!' Freshta snapped.

'Phil, I'd like to see you working out in the heat trying to disarm anti-personnel mines,' Inga voiced this with a quiet gravity that Philippe couldn't wisecrack his way out of. Emily wanted to hug her. Out of the mouths of babes. Her perfect young face was solemn. If ever there was a Human Rights archetype, she thought, it was Inga.

Mohammed stood up. 'Fuck you, Phil.' His chair clattered to the floor behind him as he left the dining room.

Oddly, this was followed by silence. Philippe looked sheepish. Above them, the light bulb dimmed again down to a filigree thread that bathed them in a creepy gloom.

Then Emily recognised the main ingredient in the stew.

'It's RABBIT!'

'Oh,' Inga squealed, 'that's disgusting!'

'Poor old Bugs,' Phil mocked.

Then Raphael popped his head in the door. 'Children, children! Some laughter, finalment! Are you finished fighting now? What about the veil, ladies? Shall we go for that argument again for a change?'

Even Freshta laughed at this effrontery, and for once allowed him to pour her a glass of Cabernet.

'If you will just cut the crap for a few minutes, s'il vous plaît, you might enjoy this splendid piece of music I have for you all!' He placed a CD in the boom box on the side table. The sound of an old Carlos Gardel Milonga filled the room, an unlikely aural balm. He was right. No one wanted to be stressed this late in the evening, with one more day at the office before the weekend.

'Nice one, Raphael,' Emily murmured, reaching for a glass. 'Do you think it would work in Helmand?'

'That's not funny,' Freshta began.

'Ah, lighten up…'

An hour later, Marisol, who had joined them when she heard the Argentinian music, was dancing Tango with Raphael in the party room and Phil had agreed to attend the deminers' handover ceremony. They'd be there for some time yet, now that the night had broken over into downtime.

Making her way across the pitch black garden to her bedroom, Emily remembered the iPod, still plugged into City Power. Too late. No tiny green glow greeted her in the room, it was fried. Dead as a Dodo, an ex-iPod. Rats.

And it's just coming up to six forty a.m. now; you're listening to the BBC World Service… The familiar clipped tones roused her from sleep. Hauling onto one elbow, she reached for her mobile phone, which already flashed a text message. It was Azad.

'Early pick-up today. C U 30mins.' Shit, she'd better get up. She showered and pulled on her red and grey selwar kameez taking in the view of the compound as she gathered her things.

She stopped a moment by the window at the sight of Baba Najib, the house grandfather, sweeping up leaves in the middle distance. He'd been the gardener in the house since the seventies, and despite the many changes down the years, he still appeared every morning to work.

The morning light fell on his wiry frame, the crags of his face deep and tired. She wondered how old he was.

Inga interrupted her thoughts then, knocking at the bedroom door. She was dressed to go out, her scarf already pulled up tight over her wild blonde hair. She was like a puppy.

'Hey, Emily. Tahir's taking me to the market early today so I can buy a nice rug. Do you want to come?'

Outside, brandishing a set of car keys, Tahir flashed a movie-star grin. Emily smiled back. Who needed George Clooney when they had Tahir?

'No, thanks, early start myself. And watch out, Inga. Don't let Security see you in Tahir's vehicle.'

'Yeah, but I'm off on home leave this Saturday, I can't go without a carpet!'

'Why, you going to fly home on it?"

'Ha ha. Too hard to get air space clearance these days..."

'Well, just let Tahir do the bargaining, okay?'

Tahir nodded. 'Come on, Miss Sweden,' he said, 'let's get you a carpet.'

As she pulled on her own scarf, Emily spotted Raphael clowning at the window of the dining room across the way, holding up a cup of coffee. He opened it and shouted over:

'Ma chère! Du café, tout prêt à boire!'

'Merci! I'm coming!'

The garden was getting busy now, with people off to work, house staff arriving , drivers at the gate. She sighed. Some days, here, she thought, despite all the shit going down, there could be sun on the rose bushes, roasted coffee smells, clear skies— yet you'd never make a Hallmark card out of it.

When Emily got to the dining room, Raphael had already gone ahead, leaving her fresh, diplomatic pouch coffee on the dining room windowsill with a saucer neatly on top. She reached for the cup, and was lifting it to her lips when the blast came.

It was the loudest, longest sound she ever heard. It was the briefest, the most chilling, and stark. The shock wave hit the window, and time itself shattered into infinitesimal fractions of its normal beat, so that she felt the weird, weird thud of the shock, heard the wood frames almost splitting just a foot in front of her face, but not quite. Glass was smashing somewhere behind her, and nearby. Eyes jammed shut, every muscle taut; for a second there was a brief limbo of silence, and then there was nothing: a blockage in time.

Then random images began flickering in murkiness: Inga and Tahir, Azad, Karim, Freshta, Monsieur Yasin, Baba Najib, Marisol, Raphael...

Everything flooded back in an onslaught, except oddly, just on one side of her head. Phones were ringing and a walkie-talkie crackled. She heard the surreal screech of a smoke alarm going off in the kitchen. For a moment, or forever, she felt like she was returning from far away, or emerging from underwater. She tried to hear what was happening outside, but sounds were distorted and sirens from the base were drowning things out, except for a man screaming and the chilling thrum of a Huey.

In a rag-doll heap on the dining room floor, she raised her shaking hands, first thought being that she was — astonishingly — intact, heart bursting. Ringing in her ears, and guts churning like rabid eels, but alive. The window in the side wall behind her had shattered inwards, but not the one she'd been facing. Lucky, lucky, she thought. You are so lucky. You are so fucking lucky.

She tried to stand up, but couldn't, a heavy feeling in the back of her head. She crawled on her knees to the window, only to see a blurred horror of confusion, a cloud of dust fluttering scarlet petals across broken glass. Every pane along the courtyard opposite had been blown back into the rooms. The roof of the pergola had gone through Raphael's window and it looked like a person was crushed between it and the casement.

She saw a man's legs. A burqa-covered body lay in the periphery of her vision, blood flowing down the path from beneath it, but though she saw the destruction, it wouldn't really compute. Nauseous, she collapsed on the floor again, and pulled herself into a sitting position against the window seat. A chopper came in low overhead, churning a pall of black, stinking smoke through the smashed pane. The room seemed to be very dark now, everything getting louder, and it struck her that she hadn't even drunk Raphael's coffee.

She stared at the long spill of it, soaking into the threadbare carpet, and was surprised to see, blending into it like an abstract painting, several splashes of rich, seething red. Well, she thought, staring. Here we are.

Reprisal.

ACACIA DREAMING

Every evening they show up at dusk, white cotton-clad, hair covered. Some with others, some alone or with kids, walking up the hill and then around the great Acacia tree, offering incantations of their faith.

A biblical tableau: the dusty earth, the empty heavens, the stone of the church nearby with towering cross stark in contrast to their quest. They are clouds of faith, vessels of prayer, clusters of sadness.

Grandmothers, mothers, widows, cowed by horror, by grief. Their whispers rise strong and timeless into the eaves of ancient branches and up the shadowing sky.

Who can say what prompts them to come here? The politicians have no fear of them. The priests remain in chapels with their books.

Dry and rainy season they return to pray and dream, perhaps, of safer times; when hope once shone in now-gone eyes and the sacrifices made were true. But with time, the conflict didn't end, just changed. So now they pray, for something beyond truth—the biggest small word in the world — peace.

As they walk they are dreaming of the dead or the absent still alive — dreaming of the bombs and guns and bullets and tanks and grenades and rockets and gas and hatchets and landmines and shrapnel and crazed warlords and gun-toting children and power-wielding leaders and government conspiracies and coups and commerce and greed and lies and madness and hunger and despair and anything else that kills their children, their husbands, their sisters, their brothers… under whatever name it's executed, in their tongue or anyone else's. Mostly in that of the hardest of small words — war.

They are as persistent and vulnerable as soft-winged moths that batter night after night at a window, called by light. They are slim figures in the refuge of the Acacia, yet they are strong and old and solid as the tree itself, their wood and leaf cathedral.

They follow their savaged hearts like mothers in distant plazas or rainy northern streets dreaming of children killed or harmed by any or all of the above: the universal bind of love in war.

They come each evening, with the cooling light under the survivor tree, to pray. It must be hard to return each day, to walk across the sand and up the hill time after time, year after year, in the knowledge that despite their prayer they still will die, in every ghastly way that words can tell.

It must be hard, to pray each evening for soldier men and women and boys and girls who went off to fight, dreaming in turn that they were fighting for the very thing their mothers pray for now.

DOGS

07:30 hours:

In early summer, a muted palette of colours made up the dust in Kabul. Brick dust, truck dust, crumbling concrete. Sometimes worse. It curled a low dance around the burnished feet of children and clung to the hems of burqas. It piled along the traffic meridians and the kerb sides. Just above the city, it hovered in a saffron-grey pall. There was always colour; in the streets around the guesthouse, bougainvillea swaggered over compound walls, the parks were filled with platoons of sunflowers, snow on the mountains crested white against eternal blue. But sometimes, driving through the city, it seemed to be smothering in a bone-hued powder. It would be good to get out into the country.

Once past the Ministry of Defence, Hanif drove towards the river and alongside it, with the old city on their right. Even this early in the morning, he had to dodge the honking cars and pick-ups that crowded the traffic lanes. Men on bicycles, APCs, buses, tinted-windowed 4Runners and donkey carts.

A motorcycle weaved past them bearing a man, a woman and two children sandwiched between them. To their left, Spring's melted Himalayan snows still flowed down the middle of the riverbed with goats and sheep grazing on either side. In a month it would be reduced to a trickle. They passed the marketplace, with its anarchic stalls offering everything from kites to songbirds, both once banned by the Taliban. Crossing the river further on, the traffic thinned and greenery began to emerge from breaks in the buildings, the structures got lower and the air began to clear. With the city behind them, the morning light had that clarity and depth that made everything seem perfectly sharp and clear.

Field trip. Were there ever two words that could lift the heart of a curfew-bound, security-regulated Kabul dweller? Emily checked her phone, and there was a text from the woman she was to accompany to the arms handover event in Ghazni province.

'Hangin' with Mahsood!' it read. Emily pondered the mysterious words. Mahsood? As they rounded a corner, she smiled at the sight of the iconic, handsome face of Ahmed Shah Mahsood, splashed all across a giant billboard at the left side of the road. Incandescent leaves, morning sun behind them, framed the hero in reflective pose, brows furrowed. Above him towered a mountain and beneath stood a young woman, smiling and garbed in a dark, Khimar-style hijab. Emily waved.

'Hi!'

'Hi, I'm Tahmina. Nice to meet you.'

The woman hoisted two large bags up into the back of the vehicle.

'The screen for the presentation...weighs a bloody ton.'

The last note of her sentence lifted up with the rich, unexpected tones of West Yorkshire. She settled into the seat.

'Newcastle!' Emily guessed.

'Bradford via Peshawar, long story.' She placed another bag behind the passenger seat.

'It's a shame emails don't do accents,' Emily said. 'I would have enjoyed them so much more.'

Tahmina's face was enveloped by the fabric of her hijab, which accentuated a glow of bare flawless skin. The rest fell tent-like as far as her waist, over the kameez that went below the knee, with the standard loose pants underneath. Interestingly, it was dark maroon, not black.

'Nice colour,' noted Emily.

'Oh, I'm a real rebel,' Tahmina replied.

Once she had settled into the back seat opposite Emily, the car built up speed and the road to the mountains improved.

'Think this is okay?' Emily was wearing a simple navy blue selwar-kameez with an embroidered panel in front and a clumsily-draped dupatta. 'The scarf has a mind of its own.'

'I'll give you a lesson,' said Tahmina. 'You need pins. Possibly a hair cap.'

Emily made a face. 'Really?'

Tahmina laughed at her. 'In this heat, right? Lightweight. It isn't so important for you, anyway. It's me that needs to be careful.'

'Were you born here?'

'Yeah. Masters in Conflict Resolution: can't cook pilau.'

'I can't cook, period,' Emily grinned. 'The York programme?'

'University of Bradford,' Tahmina said.

'Great. So you organised the whole event.'

'Well, with a just a little help from the United World Arms Decommissioning Agency.'

They laughed.

'I hear you were in Darfur.'

'Yes. Nearly two years.' Emily said.

'I was in South Sudan with UW, so my experience is mostly from there.'

'That can't have been an easy gig. What made you come here?'

'Well, after South Sudan, my options were DRC, deep field Liberia or Chad. So I went for the easy option ...' They laughed again.

She cleared her throat. 'Any questions about the event?'

'This seems like a fairly rural area. It would have been a Taliban stronghold, right?'

'Yes, definitely. It's not all-out conflict, like Helmand or Kandahar, but they're regaining power now in this part of the province. Historically, it's a community that has suffered with every change in power,' Tahmina told her. 'I mean, Ghazni was once the seat of a small empire, but you're talking these days about really tough mountain men with no trust whatsoever in civil administration. And they have a deep hatred of the military, national or foreign. That's the challenge, really.'

'It would be quite a feather in the international cap if we could make a go of it there,' Emily said.

'Yeah. The international cap is a bit off-kilter these days, though.'

'I've heard that a lot since I arrived.' Emily looked at Tahmina. 'Most people are finding it hard to keep positive.'

'And that's just the internationals.' Tahmina raised her eyebrows.

Emily was silent.

'Look, we can't be negative,' Tahmina went on. 'I mean, let's face it, you'd just crawl away and die otherwise, wouldn't you? Look at the progress we've made. If we can continue to use the tribal infrastructure as a way of building up trust community by community—we might have a chance. That is where my being from here might help, that's why I came back.'

09:30 hours:

Hanif was slowing down, gradually first and then he came to an abrupt stop, as the road ahead became jammed solid with skinny mountain goats. Try as he might, there was no room to manoeuvre the 4Runner around the herd. After speaking to the shepherds for a few minutes, he was not happy.

'We will have to wait until the goats go off the road, they say maybe two kilometres down here,' he pointed to a spot down several hairpin bends.

'We'll be late.'

Hanif said nothing, just inched along behind the goats, and Tahmina nodded at the view of the valley below.

'Look, no smog,' she said.

Immediately below them was a valley carpeted in brilliant green vegetation like an emerald lake. A river flowed across it, glinting in the sunlight like a watery necklace and mountains rose from each side like craggy guardians. Apart from the low sound of the car's engine, it was a timeless pastoral scene.

'It's beautiful,' Emily said. 'So…peaceful.'

'When I see that,' Tahmina said softly, 'I think, Genghis Khan, British Empire, Soviet invasion, The Taliban, The War on Terror... None of their glorious plans and aspirations are worth even the goat shit on that riverbank.'

Once the last of the herd of long-haired goats in front of them had disappeared up a track, Hanif began to drive along the mountain road at frightening speeds. Tahmina had already opened the computer on the exact file of the presentation she was to give at the event, ready to plug in and project as soon they arrived. She held onto it with one hand, grabbing the door handle with the other.

'Hey, Hanif,' Emily protested. 'You know, they're not going to start on time…'

10:30 hours:

But when they arrived, there were no officials outside, only the usual scattering of children and local civilians. There were three national policemen on the other side of the road, but the event attendees had already entered a gate set into the high brick wall around the District Administration Centre. Hanif parked behind the other international vehicles, took the screen and its stand out of the back and disappeared into the building.

Emily had just got out of the car as a tall man in traditional clothing and a turban was approaching the building. Half-way up the path however, he stopped and looked down at

130

the UW vehicle. He stared for a moment at Tahmina, then he walked towards them, his wooden staff thumping the ground in time with the march of his steps. Emily tried to greet him, but he ignored her, instead pulling open the kerb-side door so hard that it jammed back on itself. He began to speak in angry tones at Tahmina.

In the car interior, Tahmina touched the edge of her hijab, looked directly at the man and began to say something. He cut her off, roared something else and started to gesticulate, delivering what sounded like a sermon. A crowd was gathering around the car. The police had come over and there was a cluster of blue Burqas and older villagers. Some of the burqaed women had babies in their arms.

'Excuse me,' Emily said. The man ignored her again. When Tahmina tried to speak once more, the man raised his voice and launched into an all-out tirade. A toddler began to cry. Tahmina's lips were pursed, and there was more fear than anger in her eyes. One hand grasped the headrest of the front seat, the other scrunched a handful of her kameez tightly into her left fist, white knuckled.

Emily looked at her phone. No bloody signal. She wanted to go inside to the event and get someone, but was loathe to leave Tahmina with this maniac. Hanif came running back down the path. He looked at the man with a fear that shook Emily a little.

'Who is he? Why is he shouting at Tahmina?'

'District Administrator. Very important man. He say she bad woman. Prostitute.'

'What?'

Reaching the car, Hanif began tennis-necking from

Tahmina to the Administrator. He skipped foot to foot like a nervous hen.

'No burqa. He say where is burqa? Face not covered. Hands not covered. Not going to the event.'

'He can't stop her from going in!'

Emily inched along the side of the vehicle, but the Administrator slammed his wooden staff down on the roof of the UW vehicle, just slightly to the left of her head, with a loud crack. She gasped at the violence of it.

'Emily — stop!' Hanif hissed. 'Do not talk to him'.

The man shouted now at Emily. She could smell body odour and heavy tobacco. Some of his spit landed wetly on her right eyelid just above the lashes and she had to stop herself from raising a hand to wipe it off. A band of icy liquid steeled its way across the inside of her chest; the force of his invective felt almost physical. She stepped back. When he turned and began to address the crowd, some of the women stood to attention, others bowed slightly.

'He say nobody is help her. Punishment for look at her.'

After another loud strike on the roof of the car, the onlookers began to move away and soon were gone.

'So, where are our colleagues? Why is nobody coming out to us?' Emily glanced up the path.

'Ceremony start now,' Hanif told her.

The Administrator slammed the car door shut and turned sharply to walk up the path to the District Headquarters building. Tahmina sat back into the seat. After he had gone through the gate, there was only a blinding white calm, sun-baked and empty. Hanif's mouth was open, he looked panicked.

'Okay, quick. Take the laptop in to Christophe,' Emily told him. 'It's ready.' She placed it into his arms with a power cable and an extension chord, dumping Tahmina's printed speech on top. 'Give this to him too.'

'You come!'

'No. I'm staying here with Tahmina a bit, she's upset.' She walked a few steps up the path with him. 'So, Hanif — she can't go inside?'

'No, Emily. He say she cannot put her foot on the ground of his administration. Not even one foot.'

When the wooden gate closed behind Hanif, Emily realised she and Tahmina were alone. The national police were no longer there, the blue ghosts were all gone, children gone, old folks gone; she had never been in a rural village so deserted. It was Bergmanesque. She walked back and leaned in the window of the car.

'Listen, Tahmina, it'll be okay. I'm sure someone will be out to us in a minute, it'll be sorted. It...it's absolutely disgraceful.'

Tahmina said nothing.

Emily's phone beeped. 'Where RU?' It was Christophe messaging.

Now a signal, she thought.

'Needed ASAP!'

'Administrator has grounded Tahmina,' she tapped back. 'Pls help!'

'Event started. Just come.'

'Staying — or let's bring Tahmina in.'

'No!' Then, 'UR official photog. Needed here.'

'Per UW Gender Policy, staying as support.'

133

'Not here as Gender Off, here as Photog.' Emily fumed. She looked at the tiny screen as another text popped up. 'Do not embarrass this office.'

Emily's nose crinkled in disbelief. *What*? She couldn't believe it, not from Christophe. She looked around the plaza. A lizard blinked from a low rock beside the road. The white international cars were laid out in a line like metallic sunbathers and the only visible Afghan soul was sitting inside one of them, shaking. Emily looked at the mobile again. She switched it off.

'Hopefully they won't be too long,' she said, walking around the car to sit in beside Tahmina.

'You should go in,' Tahmina said, quietly. She was sitting in the same position as she had been when the Administrator slammed the door.

'And leave you here by yourself ? I don't think so.'

'You're not Afghan, you don't have to stay.' Tahmina glared. Her Bradford was coming back. 'Nothing will happen, believe me. He's ordered them to stay away and have nothing to do with me. I'll be fine.'

'Well, he can't order me. What I want to know is who is going to address this? They can't just leave you here!'

Tahmina didn't respond, and Emily kept talking.

'Well, they can stuff their ceremony. I can't believe this. To be honest, I have my period. I really don't feel like walking around for two hours taking pictures of any of them.'

Tahmina leaned over and put her elbows on her knees and her forehead in her hands.

'Look, maybe you'd prefer me not to stay,' Emily stammered. 'I don't want to make more of a scene than what's already happened. But maybe — I just thought — I mean, why should you stay here by yourself. They can't do this.'

'They *can* do this,' Tahmina shouted. She lifted her head, eyes glistening. 'I mean, listen to yourself! What are you thinking — they *do* do this! They do it every day. Do you think you can change the world by coming out here with a fucking scarf on your head?'

Emily said nothing.

'They've done a lot worse, Emily ... if this were six years ago I'd be in a pulp on the ground — I might even be dead.'

'I was sort of thinking that some of our international colleagues would sort it.'

'The boys in the suits? And why would they do that? Do you think this is the first time this has happened? Talk to your female Afghan colleagues — you have no idea. You think we like coming out in the field to be treated like this? When we made an official request not to be sent on field events, they didn't hold a meeting to see what could be done about it, they told us, "if you can't handle field trips you'd better find a different department".'

'My God.'

'God has nothing to do with it.'

'I'm sorry.'

'I do want you to stay...' Tahmina's voice broke a little on the last word. 'Look, a man shouted at me. So what? I'm still here and I'm fine. He didn't hurt me.'

The traditional music coming from inside the building blasted and faded suddenly, as Christophe walked out the gate and down the path. He looked like an alien was going to burst out of his chest. Calm, controlled Swiss fury.

135

'Christophe,' Emily said, 'Thank God you're…'

'Give me the camera,' he snapped, ignoring Tahmina. Emily froze.

'We'll discuss this later. For now, I need some way of covering the event.'

11:30 hours:

'Periods,' Tahmina said. 'They are our lowest common denominator.'

Emily laughed. 'That's for sure.'

'They always come at the worse time.'

'I hate these events, anyway,' Emily said. 'Sometimes you're just a ghost. And there they all are — Western and Asian both — up at some podium swinging their willies…'

Tahmina laughed out loud. 'Why should you care? I mean, you western girls — you're sort of like extra-terrestrials — they don't know what to do with you. That's why they don't expect you to wear a burqa.'

'You know, the day I arrived, there was an event at the Intercon. I was told I wouldn't need my scarf, since I was "an International." So I walked in there like this —'

She let her scarf fall off her head for a couple of seconds and Tahmina's face lit up with mirth.

'Yeah. Like that.'

She covered up the Titian mane. 'There was this Talib — my first encounter. I remember thinking, "if looks could kill, this is only my first day in the country and I am already quite dead."'

'So you *went native.*'

Emily winced. She deserved that. Just out here with a scarf on her head. 'I find it more comfortable to wear the Pakistani gear.'

'I'm not really native anymore myself. Do you know what they call us, the ones who've returned?'

'What?'

'Bottled water.'

'Really?'

'Because we grew up in Europe or America, we can't drink the water out of the tap here like everyone else. We can only drink expensive bottled stuff. So we are "bottles of water."'

'Funny.'

'You have to have a sense of humour about it.'

'Must be hard, though.'

'What's hard right now is this heat. It's got to be over thirty-eight degrees.' They were beginning to swelter. They tried running the engine and leaving on the air-conditioning, but that produced a strong smell of petrol that was nauseating. They opened the windows, but with the sun almost directly overhead, there was no shade.

12:00 hours:

By noon the windows were still open, but there was not a breath of wind. Beads of sweat rolled down Emily's face and her clothes were wet through all across her torso, under her arms and between her breasts.

They had several bottles of water, at least, but they were both swathed in dark colours, with long sleeves and covered heads. They both had worn sturdy shoes in case of rocky terrain. They removed the shoes.

Tahmina's toes, painted a delicate shade of coral, twinkled under the seat. They unfastened their bras.

'Can't we take off these selwar things?' Emily asked. 'I mean, the kameez part is basically a proper, long dress…'

Tahmina snorted. 'You have to wear the pants with it. You can't separate them, it's called a *selwar-kameez*. You wouldn't be dressed…'

'Yeah, I suppose.'

'And what if he came back, you idiot?' She began to fidget. Her face was fixed in a deep frown. She leaned back on the seat, eyes closed for a few minutes.

"My cousin died sitting in a bus at the side of the road in the sun,' Tahmina said.

'Jesus.'

'She was one of a group being taken to a healthcare workshop organised by a UW Women's Group. A mini-bus came for them — they were waiting in the marketplace, but the driver had parked away from the other cars up the road a bit. So they walked up and all piled in… ' she paused again.

'Then a few minutes later, the driver got out of the bus and walked away…'

Emily waited. Tahmina frowned in a silent, gathering back of grief.

'They couldn't get out of the bus to walk down the street — no man, you see. The driver was the official accompanying man, and he was gone. They wouldn't have known what to do.' Her words were being vacuumed back inside her, as she seemed to take breaths in without letting them out again.

'They were sitting there for ten minutes before the bus blew up. Eight women and their kids.'

'Oh, I'm so sorry.'

Tahmina leaned forward again and put her hands over her face. Deep, smothered sobs shook her body. The force of the Administrator's aggression was still ringing in Emily's head, it flooded back again as she put an arm around Tahmina's shoulder.

12:30 hours:

In the compound behind the wall, the loudspeakers were droning steadily. At one point, they adjusted the sound system and they could actually hear the words. The Mayor got up to give his speech. The District Administrator got up to give his speech. The United World representative gave his speech, and Tahmina, who had worked on her speech all week, did not get to give her speech.

'I think it's bleedin' hilarious,' she said. 'Four years at the Sorbonne, two in Bradford for an MA, two years in South Sudan and now home — to be locked up like a dog in the back of a car.'

Emily listened, and in her head, she visualised the scene inside the arms handover ceremony. Audience sitting in the cool shade of the courtyard, tea cups in hands. In front of the speakers there would be a long table covered with a white cloth, loaded up helter-skelter with a variety of arms; sometimes, it has to be said, rather old arms. She wondered whether there would be plastic explosives. Body belts. Digital devices. Even that genius, miniature death-dealer, the smartphone.

'In America,' Tahmina continued, 'they have laws about leaving a dog in the back of your car. Actual laws where the person can do jail time or get a fine. '

'Really?'

'Yeah. It's illegal to leave a dog in the back of a car in the sun. I read it somewhere after a couple in Texas fried a mastiff.'

Emily pulled her scarf up from her neck and scrunched her shoulders, trying to let a little air down her back.

'*What* are you doing?' giggled Tahmina.

'Heat itch. It's driving me nuts.'

Tahmina took a map out of the side pocket in the door of the car and began to fan them with it.

'What about your family, are a lot of them abroad now?' Emily asked.

'My mother was killed in the eighties. We were sent to stay with my aunt in Herat for two years, because my father went to fight. He left everything behind—our house and everything—and joined Mahsood. But eventually, he got us out, I don't know how.'

'So he was one of the original rebels.'

'Actually, he was an architect. You know that building beside the Ministry of Health with a facade and no back?'

'Yes.'

'He designed that. With a back.'

'Did he ever remarry?'

'My Dad? In a way. He slept with an AK-47 beside him in bed for the rest of his life. Sometimes when I would make the bed, I'd put the gun into the back of the wardrobe, but he'd just take it out again every night. He wasn't an easy man.' Her voice faltered a moment. 'What about your father?'

'He was an accountant,' Emily said. 'When I left school, he got me a job at the bank. When I got the visa for America, he wanted me to bring the bank uniform with me, because it was such good quality and might be useful for interviews with other banks.'

'Well, you're so much better off now,' said Tahmina. 'Working in a bank these days can be dangerous.'

It was beginning to really boil. They sipped their water, and after a while, they ate some samosas and oranges that the guesthouse cook had packed into a Tupperware container as a snack for Emily.

The Director of the UW Arms De-Commissioning Agency was on the podium now. He spoke of a new way forward and a different kind of brotherhood, where men would no longer need arms to survive.

There was a round of applause.

Tahmina and Emily looked at each other.

'No arms, eh?' Tahmina laughed. They began to giggle.

'Stop, please, I'm going to pee…'

'I've been wanting to pee for the last hour!'

'No peeing women allowed!'

'We're not even supposed to have the thing you're not allowed to pee with!'

'I know.' Tahmina's shoulders were shaking. 'Stop! I will really…'

'Just say three Hail Marys!' Emily snorted.

'The Virgin Mary!' Tahmina said. 'I wonder how she ever had that baby…'

13:00 hours:

Every single thing in the car was hot to touch. Emily was hot just sitting in one place, but if she moved, the plastic seat was even hotter where her body had not come between it and the sun's rays. The cotton of her garment was knotting into damp lumps that stuck into her legs and back. They sat, listless, headachy. Emily began to feel sporadic pain due to the natural urge to pass water. They decided to sit calmly and read. They sat calmly. They read.

From inside the compound, a rich, spicy smell wafted over; lunch was being served. After another twenty minutes, Emily was in real discomfort, and Tahmina was shading a twitch in her eye where a migraine threatened.

'You know, the doctors in the UW medical centre have had to treat women for serious urinary infections due to stuff like this happening on field trips. It's not natural!'

'My friend got kidney stones,' Tahmina said.

'We have to pee.'

'Maybe they'll be back soon.'

'Can't we just get out and find a house?' Emily asked. 'Wouldn't some woman let us in to go to the loo?'

'Are you mad?'

Despite the harrowing temperature, Tahmina was going pale. There were dark circles under her eyes. Suddenly, she reached forward and picked up the large square Tupperware box, now ex-samosas. It was deep, and it had a lid. They pushed the passenger seat as far forward as it could go. The whole operation was difficult and terrifying, but they managed. Afterwards, their spirits were somewhat lifted.

'You know that under Article 37c, Paragraph III, this is tantamount to abuse of official UW vehicles...' Tahmina said.

Emily began to giggle again.

'Vehicles may not be used as sanitation facilities by female staff unless Form 10B is filled out in triplicate and sent to the Chief of Transport.'

'Forty-eight hours in advance...'

'Next problem, my dear. What are we going to do with that?' Tahmina asked. She indicated the brimming Tupperware container.

'I know what I'd like to do with it...'

14:00 hours:

It was another hour before the crowd inside began to emerge from the gate. The Administrator walked with the UWADA Director and the Chief of Section, followed by the Mayor, the local Chief of Police, more international staff and former combatants. They all shook hands warmly before beginning to make their way down the path towards the cars.

'Here they come.' Emily was nauseous, she didn't open her eyes.

They were laying back, feet stretched out beneath the seats in front of them, their heads splayed against the back seat. Tahmina had stopped talking some time previously.

Emily could hear the British accent of the UWADA Director, who sounded like he was stopping a moment to speak to Christophe. Emily caught phrases of the exchange through the open window: Losing face... As if that woman didn't know to cover up… No woman's speech… to have touched the hearts and minds... No photographs… insubordination… No matter how many peace accords, you can never trust the bloody Airish.

Tahmina was holding Emily's hand, the other was lying palm up on the car seat, and part of her hijab was folded over her eyes. She was immobilised with a migraine. Apart from the samosas earlier, they had not eaten since six-thirty that morning. Emily's cheeks were cherry-flushed and burning up, she just wanted to get on the road.

She could hear people getting into cars, doors slamming, and it suddenly occurred to her that they had not met up with the main convoy on the way out, due to the goats on the road.

'Hey — do you think they just didn't know we were here, or do they not want to taint themselves, like the villagers?'

'Screw them,' muttered Tahmina, without moving her head.

Hanif scrambled up to the car.

'Are you okay?' he asked urgently when he saw them. He handed a cold bottle of water in through the back window.

'Thank you.' Emily put the bottle against her forehead.

'Are you okay?' Hanif repeated.

'Just drive please, Hanif,' Emily said. Before he started up the engine, he removed something from inside his waistcoat and handed back to Emily an amorphous, squishy looking packet wrapped in brown paper. Emily sat up too quickly, then closed her eyes as a peppering of dizzy stars ran across her vision.

'This is not look very nice,' he said. 'But I bring for you.'

She let go of Tahmina's hand and pulled apart the folds

of the paper. Inside there was a crude white plastic bag filled with aromatic pilau rice and dollops of spicy goat meat.

'Hanif, thank you so much—you are very kind.' He began to drive away as the convoy started to move.

As she lay back again, Emily caught sight of two blue ghosts staring at her from a doorway across the street. At least she thought they were staring, but she couldn't see their faces.

14:30 hours:

It wasn't until they were well up into the mountains that their bodies began to cool down, and Emily was beginning to feel human again, just about. The chill of air conditioning soothed their burqa-less souls. Ten kilometres outside the village, they had to stop. Emily held Tahmina's shoulders as she threw up the food Hanif had brought them. The white vehicles passed them by and continued on. There was no signal on her phone, but Emily guessed she wouldn't be receiving any more texts from Christophe that day.

As they continued the journey, Tahmina lay back, in a silent battle with her migraine. Emily, feeling somewhat revived by the food and water, began to chat.

'What we should do, somehow, is devise a way to airlift all the women out of the Taliban Area of Operations—every last one of them, old ladies, young girls, female babies—just get them the hell out of there. Then let those guys live all by themselves as manly men for about a year. That would sort it, really, wouldn't it?'

Tahmina didn't respond.

145

'What am I saying? A week would do it.' Tahmina still didn't react.

Emily sighed. 'Sorry, Tahmina, just kidding. But I suppose that's a bad joke.'

'No,' Tahmina whispered from under the hijab. 'That's actually… blasphemy.'

FERENJI

Maura watched the white chopper approaching with its familiar menacing growl. Menacing, or of course, reassuring, depending on the context. A soldier once told her, 'if you're a medevac, it sounds like music.' She wanted it to be reassuring, but the frown she'd woken up with still knitted her brows. Everybody now feared the drought. Except, apparently, those with the power to do something about it. The local elders and families knew they were in a fragile situation. Poor harvests and years of war had left them with neither bread nor breadwinners and now the political climate was deteriorating again.

Today the chopper was bringing a group of experts that would evaluate the need for emergency response in the province. Maura and the local staff had prepared a briefing and a short field trip.

At the perimeter fence, the village kids began to scurry into formation like a miniature crowd at a football match.

'*Ferenji! Ferenji!*' a little girl shouted, jumping up and down.

Maura laughed, and clapped her hands along with the ragged welcoming committee. The arrival of a chopper was prime local kiddy entertainment. It descended gracefully out of the African sky and their joy erupted into cheers as the wheels hit the earth. She took a breath as the dust settled enough for the door to open. Only just past 08:00, it was already thirty degrees.

The timing was ideal: an early-morning visit, before the heat of day could make the team too sleepy or uncomfortable.

Moments later, the head of the delegation, a portly Consul General, alighted. Behind him came an Italian woman, holding onto a broad-brimmed hat. A Norwegian nun came next, all perfect skin and gentle eyes, followed by a white-haired American and a West African man in a traditional robe.

Eventually the party stood, smiling and nodding, in a small group in the shade of the helicopter.

'Welcome!' Maura said. 'My name is Maura Redmond, and I'm the Project Officer here for BUA, the NGO selected to show you around a little bit. These are my Zohmean colleagues, Paolo, who will translate for us, and Luul, our Project Assistant.'

They shook hands.

'We've prepared a presentation and a trip to a local village,' she continued.

'Thank you,' the West African said. 'We are looking forward to it.'

'What does BUA stand for?' the Italian woman asked.

'It means "victory" or "success" in the Irish language.'

'As in the war on poverty?'

For a split second, Maura thought she was kidding.

"As in the work we do with local communities providing what we can to facilitate sustainable living.'

'But no drought in Ireland, eh?' the Consul said.

'No, plenty of rain there,' Maura said. 'Nobody knows how much I miss it sometimes.' The group laughed.

'So,' said a man who introduced himself as a Humanitarian Liaison Officer with U.S. Outreach. 'We have reviewed the funding proposal you submitted — can I take it that you are the one who prepared it?' He indicated a crisp document, folded neatly in his hand. It was so crisp that it struck Maura he'd only read it on the flight up. 'It makes rather grim reading...'

'Yes, that's why we're so glad to see you all,' Maura said. 'The vehicles are just over here, we'll get back to the BUA house, and when you're ready we'll have the briefing and then head out for a visit.

That way you'll have an opportunity to observe the situation on the ground for yourselves.'

On the drive back to the office Maura's face fell back into a frown. She reminded herself not to expect too much from the day. They'd been waiting months for this delegation. Over the previous six weeks, there had been countless emails — all in the polite, unemotional language of the organisation, necessary to attract attention without causing too much alarm.

> *Would like to advise that conditions have not improved since last report. The shipment of food and medicines authorised in your memo 6th May last has not arrived, and port officials are not responding to queries. Would appreciate immediate investigation of shipment's status, and/or despatch of new shipment.*

'Thanks for your email, Maura. Awaiting word from port admin our end and will revert.'

She always drafted her reports late at night in the office, alone. Mostly because she was prone on occasion to weep as she wrote. They were too emotional, full of the gutted expressions on farmers' faces as they surveyed their fruitless land (community members manifesting distress), the terrified eyes of mothers watching their babies being weighed and evaluated (statistics reveal increasing malnutrition among infant population), or the lines of ragged souls outside the field hospital, some having walked for days to get there (pronounced influx of refugees).

There was a theory among her United World colleagues that routine field reports were not even read by their HQ. Legend had it that a Swiss volunteer working in South Sudan once sent off a Weekly wherein he'd globally replaced the word 'refugees' with the word 'raspberries' and HQ didn't pull him up on it for six months, by which time he was in Congo with a news agency.

It was a good story, but no consolation for Maura, who tapped controlled fury and frustration onto her keyboard, leaving off every now and then to let her eyes un-blur. She relegated initial versions to the drafts folder. The following morning, she'd revise the text, replacing any purple prose with understated reason before clicking 'send'.

Five miles away, in a sloping field near the edge of the escarpment, Makda carefully poured a precious cup of water into one end of a beehive, making sure not to anger the

Queen, and not to let the container overflow. The bees loved their sweet water. She moved along each hive and repeated the motion, their low buzzing like a quiet song in the haze of the morning.

Muted voices from the other huts floated up on the thin air as she worked. A cloud shadow moved across the valley below, deepening the terrain's greens and blues and ochres in its path. Around it, the mountains were brighter now since she had started her work. She looked at the sun. Bringing the water vessel back to the shed, she quickened her movements. The tension in her shoulders foreshadowed the day ahead.

'Mama!' Bilen was standing at the edge of the enclosure, a little cactus pear juice running down her face.

'Yes?'

'The helicopter landed.'

'Have you fed the chickens?'

'Yes, mama. Paolo is coming with Maura.'

'I know, Bilen. I am going to talk to the visitors for her. I'll give you your clean dress.'

As Chair of the Widows' and Mothers' Association, the duty of spokesperson fell on Makda naturally, although, like most of the villagers, she had a resistance to outsiders encroaching on their affairs.

The Irish woman had lived and worked with them since the end of the war, though. She meant well.

'Mama, have we honey for them?'

'Yes, I have a pot.'

'But we shouldn't give it to them, Mama. Tesfaye's uncle says there will be no honey this year.'

'We'll have lots of honey, Bilen.'

'But we have to pray for rain first.'

Makda took her daughter's hand as they walked back to their hut.

Her baby was no longer a baby. And smart; speaking English already at ten.

'Mama, the *ferenji* who are coming today—Maura says that they'll give us help again if rain doesn't come.'

'We'll see,' Makda said. While the work of the international organisations had been good for them, she understood that their money, like the red soil on the escarpment, was beginning to dry up. Today was important.

Back in the office, Maura was finishing her part of the presentation. Looking at the visitors, their teacups almost empty in front of them, her worst fear was that she was not reaching them.

'When you visit the local community, they will probably tell you they've been waiting three years for rain,' she said. 'This is not, as the figures show, an exaggeration. Rainfall levels each year for the last three years have only been between five and ten percent of the annual average for the previous decade. When we tell you that drought is imminent, the reality is that in certain places, the drought is already there—but not yet at levels that are life threatening on a large scale.'

She was speaking as clearly as she could, but the Consul appeared to be more concerned with the Indian army first aid poster on the wall, from a peacekeeper workshop earlier that month.

'Populations located along the tarmac roads — perhaps understandably — tend to get more attention from the aid community, while isolated areas like this one are struggling more each day. The fact is that people here have become almost completely dependent on international aid,' she continued. 'So now that The World Nutrition Group food and medical shipment is overdue, it's crucial that we get it.'

'What about your contingency funds?' the West African inquired.

Luul responded to this one. 'We bought emergency rations with our contingency funds three weeks ago, and although the United World Crisis Group sent a little more to help, the main shipment we were promised has not arrived. So our funds for this year are now gone.'

'And you are proposing, Ms Redmond?'

'For the long term,' Maura said, 'BUA proposes to continue working with the communities to start planning more drought resistant crops and to improve watershed management for the area.

But in the immediate future, my suggestion, as I've indicated in my emails, is to resend the shipment, or have supplies air-dropped into the area to avoid a full scale humanitarian crisis.'

There was a pregnant pause. Air-drops. Crisis. Full-scale. Their scepticism was almost tangible. The ceiling fan clacked quietly as it revolved overhead, and Maura could feel a trickle of sweat go down her back.

After a moment the Consul broke the silence. 'Well, that's what the Emergency Evaluation Committee in Prague will determine after they've considered our report, Ms Redmond. Thank you for your presentation.'

When the visitors arrived at the village, the elders and the District Administrator were waiting to greet them. They accompanied the international group on a small tour of the community given by a young teacher. By the time they arrived at Makda's hut, she had washed and dressed the three children in their best, and was waiting for them in front of it. Maura approached with a smile, greeting Makda in Zohmean. The rake-thin Bee Keeper shook hands with the visitors, and little Bilen introduced herself to them proudly in English.

They walked up to the beehives, and Maura set the interview going, with Paolo translating.

'We asked BUA to help us with the bee-keeping because it is what we know how to do, traditionally,' Makda told them. 'They brought us the new hives, which are more efficient, and we have learned about the newer methods. We have planted new bushes and trees around that have flowers to feed the bees.'

'What happens to the honey once you have made it?' the Norwegian nun asked.

'We are part of a cooperative system,' Makda continued through Paolo. 'We have a small processing unit where we crush the combs and produce the honey, and from there it goes to a bigger centre thirty kilometres from here where they can package the honey and the wax and bring it to market in the city.'

This time, the visitors seemed impressed. They looked around the apiary, where Makda showed them the crumbling old hives, made with wooden logs, wattle and straw and the new box hives. They kicked through mounds of corn cobs, traditionally used for smoking the bees; they tasted the honey from Makda's jar.

'Smokey!' the West African smiled.

'The traditional raw smoke method is being used less now,' Maura explained. 'And the processor has a temperature control so that the honey remains pure and isn't burned.'

Makda watched with some satisfaction as the honey was sampled by the group, and then she spoke again.

'Now, in the highlands, it is "small harvest" time,' Paolo translated. 'And later in the year there will be another harvest, but there is a problem because of no rain. The bees are dying. The plants are not flowering and the bees need a lot of water to make good honey and to cool the hive inside. The peacekeepers have been bringing water, but the fighting has started again, and nobody knows how long more they will be able to deliver it.'

'What Makda is saying here is all part of what the whole area is experiencing now because of the drought,' Maura said.

'Drought mean no rain!' pronounced Bilen, recognising the word.

Makda then made some more observations through Paolo, unsmiling.

'Planting seasons have come and gone, with bad harvests. No husbands to help us because of the war, and landmines in the fields. We are afraid that the hunger that happened before will come again and we will die.'

There was a moment's silence. Maura said nothing.

'How can it be possible that there's no rain?' the American asked.

'Well, right now, it's July,' Maura answered. 'We should be having heavy rainfall here on a daily basis. In the capital, it's lashing every afternoon by around three o'clock — right?'

He shrugged in agreement.

'Climate change has caused the rains to fall further north of this belt each year,' the Norwegian sister said. 'So communities who have lived in this area for generations are no longer able to depend on the seasonal weather.'

'That's it,' Maura said. 'It's on record. So literally, the villages all along the escarpment are just waiting for the rain. There's little food. No water for the animals. No flowers for pollination, no bees for honey to sell in the city co-op. A domino-effect, if you like, on the ecosystem.'

She couldn't help the emotion that spilled into her voice. 'The result is that the few development organisations here are all severely strained and under-resourced, and the communities are frankly at the end of their tether.'

There was another few moments' silence. Makda was concerned at Maura's tone. Maybe she had said the wrong thing — offended the foreigners by being forthright. She issued an instruction to Bilen, who ran quickly into their hut and began bringing out what Maura recognised as the original vessels in which the previous year's food aid had been delivered.

Makda patted flat some sacking and arranged on it a row of containers, once filled with lentils, flour, cooking oil or rice, cleaned out and gleaming in the sunshine. Last, but getting pride of place, was an almost-empty jerry can of water. She was muttering under her breath, and Bilen began to translate.

'Mama say look all the beautiful thing from international.'

Maura looked at the elders, whose faces were stony and proud.

Makda indicated the array of vessels with her hands, and continued to speak, glancing up at the visitors and down again. Paolo took up the interpretation.

'All the women in the village thank you for last year's donations, but we need your help again, please. Please take a look at what good care we have taken of them…'

This was almost unbearable. Paolo shot Maura a look that said, "who are these people?"

Maura shook her head and was about to address the group when she saw, contrary to her expectation, a half circle of stricken expressions. The American spoke.

'They're all empty.'

'Finally,' Maura said to herself.

'Empty mean no food!' Bilen beamed. The mother pulled her daughter over beside her, putting an arm around her shoulder. Maura blinked and straightened up.

'This is where all your emails start from. And where all your donations end up. This is it. I hope you can make HQ understand.'

'Don't worry, my dear,' the Consul said. His tone made her heart sink all over again. 'We'll make sure it's all quite clear in our report.'

Just an hour later she was at the edge of the helipad, straining against repeated blasts from the quickening rotors of the chopper, eyes half-closed, hair flying. Paolo had taken the other vehicle back to the office, but she stayed to take leave of the visitors. The Norwegian nun smiled at her from a porthole.

'Hey sister!' she screamed through the roar. 'You have perfect skin!'

The nun smiled back and waved a little more emphatically, then turned back into the cabin, fingers in her ears as the volume and pitch of the blades built up.

The craft began its sexy little dance between air and ground, shuddered, rose tail to the sky at first, evened out, then careened up and forward in the direction of the capital. Maura watched until it became a five-pinned speck in the sky, and then stood a while longer just looking out over the glare of the mountains, heat-shimmering and arid, beautiful in their stark, eternal way. As she put her hat back on, she observed how the saffron earth churned up by the chopper had filled in all the cracks in her field boots. She kicked one foot up and watched the dust scatter.

At home by this hour, she thought, the early train would have left for Dublin and the dawn mist would be lifting from the marsh just across from the old bridge. Sun would be filtering through the canopy of oaks and sycamores onto the broad Slaney as it flowed around the bend and south through the town on either side. Downstream, the morning light would be dancing up the estuary from the sea, scattering over the land, still drenched in dew. It might even be raining.

– fin –

ACKNLOWLEDGEMENTS

Acknowledgements are due to the following publications in which versions of these stories first appeared: *Census 2 Anthology* (Seven Towers Publishing, 2010); *Natural Bridge* (University of Missouri, St Louis); *Make Them Visible* (Oxfam Ireland, 2015); *The Review of Post-Graduate Studies* (NUIG, 2003); and *The Scaldy Detail* 2013.

'The Package Man' and 'Blue Tarpaulin' were shortlisted for Hennessy New Irish Writing Awards in the categories of fiction and poetry respectively; and 'Mare Rubrum' was shortlisted for the Francis MacManus Literary Award in 2011. 'Dogs' was shortlisted for Short Story of The Year in the An Post Irish Book Awards, 2017.

The first edition of this book *Ferenji and other stories*, was published by Doire Press, an award-winning literary press based in Galway, Ireland.

The author would like to thank The Arts Council of Ireland, for the bursary she received to complete this book.

THANK YOU

Thanks to Angela Rauch, Anna Little, Anne Flynn, Anne Doyle, Asma Rahimi, Cíarán Carty, Colonel William Gibson, Catherine Byrne, CJ Hendrix, Colum McCann, Columba O'Dowd, Dermot Bolger, Doug Mulkerns, Dru Wall, Eamonn Wall, Elizabeth Hutcheson, Elizabeth Whyte, Emer Martin, Ewa Neumann, Gai Griffin, John Walsh, Johnathan Williams, Lisa Frank, Leila Blacking, Martin Malone, Lorcan Healy, Luiz Carlos da Costa (1949-2010), Narimah Jalaludin, Nora Mannion, Orlaith Carmody, Patricia Connelly, Patrick McCabe, Peter Murphy, Phil Lewis, Ruth Ficare, Sarah Bannan, Susan Lanigan, Svetlana Peronko, Vanessa O'Loughlin, Susan McKeon, Val Mulkerns and Zoë Castillo.

Special thanks to all dear friends and colleagues with whom I worked in Central America, Africa and Afghanistan and in memory of those who have lost their lives in the service of international peacekeeping.

ABOUT THE AUTHOR

HELENA MULKERNS' debut short story was short-listed for the Hennessy New Irish Writing Award. Over two dozen of her stories have since been internationally anthologised in books and other publications, including one that was short-listed for the Pushcart Prize and another for the Francis MacManus Short Story Award.

She originally worked as a music journalist with *Hot Press* Magazine and went on to write for *The Irish Times, The Irish Echo, Publisher's Weekly and The New York Times,* among others. She worked as a press officer and photographer in UN Peacekeeping Operations in Central America, Africa and Afghanistan. She holds an MA in English Literature and Publishing from the National University of Ireland Galway, and has edited two literary anthologies: *Turbulence* (Tara Press, 2013) and *Red Lamp Black Piano* (Tara Press, 2013).

See more at the author's website: www.HelenaMulkerns.com

451
Editions

www.451Editions.com